TO YIELD TO A HIGHLANDER

THE SUTHERLANDS OF SEA CLIFF, BOOK 3

CALLIE HUTTON

Copyright © 2023 by Callie Hutton

All rights reserved.

No part of this book may be reproduced in any form or by any electronic or mechanical means, including information storage and retrieval systems, without written permission from the author, except for the use of brief quotations in a book review.

ABOUT THE BOOK

This could be the best mistake of his life...

Laird Duncan Grant doesn't want his neighboring clans, the MacIntoshes and the MacPhersons, to form an alliance by the planned marriage between their offspring. It would make for a dangerous situation for his clan. Since he is in need of a wife, he decides to seize the bride on her way to the wedding and keep her for himself.

But he takes the wrong lass.

Lady Elsbeth Johnstone is tired of living in her twin sister's shadow. She loves her dearly, but it is time for her to have her own life. With no prospects for marriage, she decides a convent in Perth is the place for her.

In the dead of night on her trek to Perth, she is dragged away from her escort by a band of men who think she is someone else. Furious at how her life is now out of her control again, she demands Laird Grant bring her to the convent in Perth.

Angry at the mistake he made, he agrees, but he can't help but wonder if he could tame the spirited lass and convince her to stay.

After all, he is in need of a wife.

1

June 1656
Dornoch Castle, the Highlands

The time had come.

Elsbeth stared into the looking glass in her bedchamber at Dornoch Castle, the home of her twin sister, Ainslee, and brother-by-marriage, Laird Haydon Sutherland.

'Twas also the home of the laird's brother, Conall, and his wife, Maura. The two pairs were well on their way to producing the necessary heirs and future warriors for the clan. Both couples were in love, blissfully happy, and tried their best to make her feel like part of the family.

She was not.

Oh, she had her place in the clan. She helped with the kitchen and garden and had been training for a while with the clan healer, Dorathia.

Ainslee had pushed various men in her direction, hoping a spark would ignite something. Were she to marry, she wanted what Ainslee and Maura had. Love. Devotion. Respect.

No man in the clan prompted those feelings in her.

She'd had a fancy for Conall from the time she'd met him when he and his brother had come to Lochwood Tower, her clan's home, to choose either her or Ainslee as a wife. 'Twas to be an advantage for both clans. Haydon had chosen her, but she'd been terrified of the man. He was so braw, loud, and arrogant. After much panic on her part, Ainslee had stepped into her place at the wedding.

The conflict that started had been resolved, and everyone agreed that Ainslee was a much better match for the laird.

Conall had been nice to her and didn't frighten her as his brother had. That kindness had continued once they'd all settled at Dornoch Castle. Ainslee had gotten permission from their da for Elsbeth to remain with her until she felt settled, since the twins had never been separated before.

She'd imagined herself married to Conall even though he'd professed to never marry. The man had a reputation with the lasses and didn't want his lifestyle to be any different. She'd hoped he would one day change his mind.

And he had.

'Twas quite a surprise and a disappointment when she'd returned from a visit with her da at Lochwood Tower to find Conall married. She'd felt adrift since then, even though Maura was a lovely lass and she and Conall made a wonderful couple.

And now they had twin lads to raise.

She checked her appearance in the looking glass, and, taking a deep breath, left the room to find Haydon to present her case.

As usual in the early hours of the morn, Haydon was in his solar, going over all the things the laird of a huge clan had to deal with. She hoped he wasn't so busy that he could not give her time. She'd made her decision, and she wanted to move forward before she lost her nerve.

A soft knock on the door resulted in a, "Come," from inside. She opened the door and breathed a sigh of relief that he was alone and not in the middle of some sort of meeting with Conall. This was something she had to do when there was no one except her and her laird present.

"Good morn, Elsbeth," the laird said.

"And to you as well," she returned.

He waved to the chair in front of his desk. "Please have a seat." He leaned his forearms on the desk. "What can I do for ye?"

Now that the time had come, she was nervous. Not that she intended to change her mind, but she knew she was in for an argument. And Haydon's argument would be one of many from others, she was sure.

She hesitated. Should she blurt it out? Or do a build-up of sorts? Now that she was facing him, her courage had begun to slip. Then she chided herself. She could never do what she hoped and planned to do if she started to have doubts. She'd spent many a night tossing in her bed thinking about this.

She cleared her throat. "I want to join a convent."

There, the words were out. As was the huge breath she'd been holding. She didn't give a big explanation; that would allow an argument. She simply stated what she wanted.

Expecting outrage, or even an immediate nay from Haydon, he surprised her by leaning back in his chair, his elbows on the armrest, his fingers tented as he tapped his lips, staring at her. "Why?"

How much to tell him? The sorrow she felt as she watched her sister cuddle and offer her breast to her new bairn? The slight bit of envy—she had finally admitted it to herself—when she saw the way Conall watched Maura as if she were the most important person in the world to him?

Should she reveal the nights of tossing in her bed, trying to convince herself that she was needed in a clan where everyone had their place and she seemed to be just an extra with no real position? She had her pride and sounding like a spoilt child, angry because everyone had a biscuit except her, would never do.

She raised her chin and met Haydon's eyes. "I have given this a great deal of thought. I feel as though I have a calling and should be serving others for the Lord."

"Ye are serving us here."

"Nay." She hated the bitterness that she heard in her voice. "Anyone else can do what I do here." She leaned forward. "I have been corresponding with Sister Albert in Perth. I met her on the trip home from my da's castle. She owns property that she inherited and houses several other nuns. They help the poor, sick, and orphans. They are doing wonderful work."

Haydon's brows rose. "I doona understand, lass. I thought there were no more abbeys or convents in Scotland anymore since the Catholic religion was outlawed?"

Elsbeth shook her head. "Nay. There are still a few scattered around, mostly in the Highlands. They keep to themselves and do good work." She straightened her shoulders. "And I wish to join them."

"Yer sister will not approve."

"I ken that. But 'tis my life, and I wish to live it the way I see fit." Most of her life had been decided by others. As much as she loved her sister and it would truly break her heart to leave her, 'twas Ainslee who had directed both of their lives over the years.

Her da wrote to her on occasion, reminding her of her duty to marry and have bairns. She couldn't understand why. Any bairns she produced would not help Da since the Johnstone clan needed a male heir. But, again, someone else trying to direct her life.

She was a woman grown and able to make her own decisions. And this was one of them.

"I ken how ye feel, lass, but are ye certain this is how ye want to spend the rest of yer life? Ye are a beautiful woman, young, smart, and with a sweet way about ye. Why would ye want to lock yerself away?"

Why indeed? Was she hiding? Surrendering? Nay. She'd given this a lot of thought and 'twas the right path for her.

"I doona see it as locking myself away, Laird. I want to help people who need it, who have no one else to turn to. I want to make a difference in one small part of the world."

Haydon shook his head. "I canna give ye my blessing, but I won't deny ye an escort to Perth. However, I think ye should speak with Ainslee about this before ye make final arrangements."

"I intend to. I just wanted to be sure ye would not deny me."

He offered her a warm smile. "Nay. 'Tis sad that women have so little choice in their life. 'Tis happy I am that yer sister is content with her life."

Elsbeth nodded, a slight stab to her heart. "Aye. She is verra happy with the bairns." She hesitated for a moment.

"And ye, too." She could feel the blush rising to her cheeks, along with the tears threatening.

He grinned like a well-pleased man. "Aye."

Had she made a mistake in allowing Ainslee to take her place at the wedding? Would she be as happy as her sister if she'd gone through with the marriage? 'Twas true that Haydon was not the horrible beast of a man they both thought when he'd arrived at Lochwood Tower to choose a bride.

She shook those thoughts off. Her sister was happy, and that was important to her. She would find her own happiness in serving others.

"I suggest ye speak with yer sister. I ken she will have objections, and ye will want to get them out of the way before ye begin yer trip."

Elsbeth nodded. "Aye. I will do that now."

As she stood to leave the room, Haydon said, "Are ye sure ye want to do this, Elsbeth? In all the time ye've been here, isna there anyone in the clan that's caught yer eye?"

She thought briefly of Conall and shook her head. "Nay."

'Twas probably best to get this done before she lost her nerve. She had to laugh because she never thought she'd see the day when speaking with her sister was more frightening than doing so with Haydon.

"HAVE YE LOST YER MIND, sister? Leave a comfortable home here to live in a convent?" Ainslee's shock was to be expected, and Elsbeth had thought she was prepared for it. But it still rocked her.

"'Tis what I feel is my calling."

"Yer calling? Ye are three and twenty years and just now ye feel the call?"

"I doona want to argue about this, Ainslee. Ye have yer life here, and a happy life it is. 'Twas the best decision ye made when ye offered to take my place with Haydon."

Ainslee collapsed onto the bed from where she'd just risen after catching up on sleep with the new bairn keeping her awake nights. She reached out and took her sister's hand, tugging her alongside her. "Are ye so unhappy, Elsbeth?"

She lifted her chin. "Nay. I just want to be of service to those who need it."

"I need ye, sister."

"Nay. Ye doona. Ye have yer husband, yer bairns, a keep to run, and Maura, yer sister-by-marriage." She shook her head, fighting desperately to keep the tears that had formed in her eyes from falling.

She raised her palm, staving off any words of comfort her sister was about to say. "Doona pretend the keep willna run smoothly if I leave." She quickly wiped the tears that had fallen, the lump in her throat as big as a boulder.

Taking Ainslee's hand in hers, she said, "I love ye. As ye ken, we have an attachment like no other. I will miss ye with my whole heart, but this is something I have to do for myself. I need a life too. And it isna here."

Elsbeth could see the fight leave her sister as Ainslee's shoulders slumped. "Aye. Ye do have the right to the life ye want." She reached out and tucked a loose curl behind Elsbeth's ear. "I'm just no' sure yer life is a convent."

Elsbeth hopped up. They were going in circles, and she had plans to make, clothes to pack, and things she no longer needed to give away. 'Twould be a busy day.

She leaned over and hugged her sister, then left as quickly as possible since she was about to fall into a blubbering heap right next to her on the bed.

It took two days for her to pack and prepare to leave. Conall tried to talk her out of it. Maura attempted the same. Dorathia tried, as did her niece, Helen. Haydon's cousin Malcolm even offered to marry her. She smiled, thanked him, and shook her head no.

By the time her last night at the keep arrived, she had what she considered a permanent headache. And heartache. 'Twould be so easy to say she changed her mind and make everyone happy, but 'twould also not be long before she hated herself and was right back where she'd been for the last few years.

Ainslee had requested that Jonet, the cook in the keep, make a special meal for supper. All of Elsbeth's favorite foods. She was beginning to believe she should have left a note and snuck out in the middle of the night, except she could never travel to Perth by herself without getting lost, or possibly killed.

So, suffering through the final meal with the family had to be done.

"Ah, lass, yer looking quite fine tonight," Malcolm said as he sat alongside her.

The hair on the back of her neck rose. Was he trying to woo her since she'd turned him down? Had Haydon or Ainslee put him up to this?

"Thank ye, Malcolm. Ye are looking quite fine as well." She turned to Donella, seated on the other side of her. The laird's sister was seldom seen in the keep. She was a shadow who appeared, then disappeared. When the keep was under her control before Haydon had married Ainslee, the place was a disaster. She was a sweet lass, but 'twas accepted that she had never grown into a woman in her mind.

"How are ye today, Donella?" Elsbeth asked.

"I am fine. I hear ye are leaving to join a convent." 'Twas probably the longest sentence the lass had ever uttered to Elsbeth.

"Aye. I leave in the morn."

"Oh." She picked up her cup of ale and took a sip. "Be careful." With those cryptic words, she smiled and began to eat from her trencher.

"I would like to walk with ye after supper, Elsbeth." Malcolm drew her attention.

God's bones, nay. There was only one reason he wanted to walk with her after supper, and she had already politely, but firmly, turned him down. The man didn't want to marry her. He was only feeling sorry for her, or maybe he was simply willing to sacrifice himself in the name of loyalty to his cousin.

"I'm afraid that is no' possible, Malcolm. I have many things to do tonight to prepare for my leave tomorrow."

"Ah, aye, yer leave."

As if he didn't remember it.

The meal couldn't be over soon enough. She did have some last-minute things to do, but the mood on the dais was somber enough that one would think she was dying instead of moving onto another life that suited her better.

Did it suit her better?

She put a quick halt to that thought. Her mind was made up. Walks with Malcolm, talks with Ainslee, and advice from Haydon would not change her mind. The sooner she left the table and retired to her bedchamber, the better for her mental state.

She rose and looked over at Ainslee. "If ye will excuse me, there are some things I need to do to prepare for tomorrow."

"Aye. I will stop by yer bedchamber before I retire."

Elsbeth nodded, and before she left the dais, Haydon said, "Be ready at dawn, Elsbeth. I'm sending about a dozen men with ye."

She nodded and left the great hall, not looking back. 'Twas something she needed to do from now on.

Not look back.

THINGS WERE NO BETTER, and possibly worse, when the morn arrived, and Elsbeth joined the team of men who were to escort her.

The weather was damp, with a slight mist shrouding them all. Despite it being summer, Elsbeth shivered in her plaid, then swung the fur-lined cloak that Ainslee had made for her over her shoulders, bringing some warmth. She knew, however, that the cold inside her would not be assuaged with a warm cloak.

Haydon, Ainslee, Maura, Conall, and Malcolm had all risen early to see her off. Another night of tossing and turning had left her weak, tired, and something she never was—peevish.

Malcolm walked up to her and took her hand in his. "Can I change yer mind, lass? Are ye sure?"

If only she could feel something for the man besides friendship. He was a strong, braw warrior with a kind heart. He would be a good husband and father to any bairns he produced. But she felt nothing when he held her hand.

"Aye. I'm sure."

He leaned over and kissed her on her cheek. "If ye change yer mind, I'll come for ye."

She nodded and turned to Haydon and Ainslee. Her sister's eyes were swollen and red, and she hated knowing that she was the cause of it. But she would be fine. Her husband stood with his arm around her shoulders, protective and loving, and she had two sweet bairns to take care of.

She took a shuddering breath. 'Twas time to end the suffering for all of them. She stepped forward and hugged Haydon, then turned to her sister and pulled her in for a hug. The tears on both their cheeks mingled, as had their lives since before they were born.

Eventually, Haydon had to pull them apart. Moving swiftly, he lifted Elsbeth and placed her on her horse.

"God go with ye, lass." He stepped back and gave a signal to the man leading the group, and they moved ahead.

She didn't look back.

She would only look forward.

2

Freuchie Castle
Home of Clan Grant

"I'm afraid we have no choice, Laird." Owen Grant thumped his knuckles on the desk in front of Duncan, Laird of Clan Grant. "Ye have to stop this. Ye canna allow this marriage to take place. If MacPherson's daughter weds the MacIntosh son, 'twill give them strength that will be a danger to our clan."

Laird Duncan Grant sat back and listened to his second-in-command. They'd just received word from one of their spies that an alliance had been forged between MacPherson and MacIntosh via marriage between their offspring.

Duncan had hoped to make the match himself to the MacPherson lass since he'd been urged continuously by his advisors to find a bride and get some heirs on her. Marriage to the MacPherson's daughter would secure the line and give them a strong alliance. The Grants had always gotten along with the MacPhersons and the MacIntoshes, despite the few raids they pulled on each other's borders.

However, the strength of the two clans together could wipe them out if they wished since the Grant clan bordered the two others. A few years before, the Grants had allied themselves with the Earl of Huntly which led to the annihilation of the Clan Farquharson, but this new threat was troublesome.

Truth be told, Duncan was tired of the constant threats. He was a warrior, born and raised to fight. He and his men trained daily, and he acquitted himself well on the battlefield, but many times he wished they would all just get along and tend to their own clans so he could settle down with a wife and raise a few bairns.

Although he was quite sure he already knew what Owen had deemed necessary to deal with this new threat, he asked anyway. "What is it ye are proposing, Owen?"

He stood up straight and crossed his arms over his chest. "I say we capture the lass, and ye marry her yerself. 'Twould anger MacPherson, no doubt, but once his daughter is married to ye he would have to accept it, and things would be better for us having an alliance with the laird."

Owen winked at Duncan. "Especially if ye get a bairn on her posthaste."

'Twas something he'd considered himself once he heard about the possible nuptials between the two. To have a bride from such a strong clan brought to his castle, ready to wed. He could have the priest marry them immediately, take the lass to his bedchamber to consummate the marriage, and 'twould be finished. Unable to be undone.

"Aye. 'Twould probably frighten the lass to be taken from her escort and brought here, but marriage to one mon or another doesn't make a difference." He waved a dismissive hand at the idea of a lass caring about who she married. "And 'twill be the best way to protect us."

Owen nodded. "Aye. And possibly the lass too. I heard the MacIntosh son is a nasty sort. She'd be better off with ye since ye are a fine mon, and after she settles down, she would be happy with ye."

They knew nothing of the MacPherson lass except what they'd heard from those who had met her at court. She was a bonnie lass, deep green eyes, straight white teeth, smooth silky skin, and red curly hair. He would certainly not have a hard time bedding the lass.

"I suggest we take a small group of men with us. I ken MacPherson will have a strong escort for the lass, mayhap even himself since there will be a wedding. 'Tis best if we avoid any sort of a clash, just grab the lass and head straight back here. I would prefer avoiding an all-out war, which would result if many of her escorts were killed."

The next morn, six men rode out of the castle walls with Duncan leading them. He'd left Owen in charge of the keep while he was gone. Things had been peaceful for a while, and even though this might rile the two clans, he didn't believe it would cause more than a skirmish when their deed was uncovered.

Duncan had been laird of the Grant clan since he'd reached seventeen summers. As the only son of Laird Kerr Grant, Duncan had been thrust into the role much too soon. Well trained as a warrior, he hadn't expected to serve as laird so young.

His da had been a young, strapping man with many years ahead of him when he was struck down in a battle and bled to death on the field before Duncan had even known.

Due to the risky nature of a Highlander's life, Kerr had set up an advisory group of men from the clan to act on his behalf should his unexpected death occur before Duncan was old enough to deal with the clan by himself.

Had it not been for the advisory group, Duncan was certain the clan would have been in a mess. Now, at eight and twenty years, he felt he was a confident, fair, honorable leader, well respected by all members of the clan as well as the other clans.

Fighting the number of battles he'd participated in had left him scarred and weary of fighting. He was particularly sensitive over the scar on his right cheek which had resulted from too close of an encounter with another warrior's sword. He kept a close beard to cover it, taking much teasing from his men for being sensitive about the scar.

Aye, mayhap he was. He'd always been a handsome man, with enough charm to enjoy plenty of lasses' attention. But he was ready to eschew all of that and join with one woman for the rest of his life. If what they'd heard about the MacPherson lass was true, getting bairns on his bride would be a pleasure, not a chore.

Waylaying a lass headed to her wedding was not unheard of in the wilds of the Highlands. Duncan had just never expected to be one of those lairds who resorted to such tactics.

The group traversed the most likely path that the group escorting the bride from the MacPherson land to the MacIntosh clan would take. They rode most of the time at night, carefully making their way in the woods, keeping off the main path, not wanting to be seen by anyone traveling the road through the clans.

Towards the middle of the second night, Duncan held up

his hand as a signal for the men to stop when he heard the mumbles of low conversation. Once they stopped, he jumped from his horse. "I will see if this is our group and what the layout is."

John, one of his men, nodded.

Duncan walked as far as he could without being seen, careful not to step in a small animal hole or crunch twigs and leaves. Wee animals scattered from his path as he made his way, and an owl hooted from his perch above him. His night vision was very good, so the lack of full moonlight didn't deter him.

He soon saw a small campfire that kept about ten men surrounding it warm in the damp woods. There was no sign of a lass, but just as he decided 'twas not the group they were waiting for, a young woman rose from behind a man who had been blocking her from his sight.

Duncan sucked in a deep breath. This had to be their lass. Beautiful, slender, long red curly hair. She smiled at one of the men, and his blood raced to his groin. Aye, he'd have no problem bedding this lass.

She made her way past the other men who seemed to hold her in high regard, no lewd remarks or leering looks. Aye, that sort of respect would be expected for a laird's daughter. She moved to a tent that had been set up not too far from where the men no doubt would sleep near the fire.

He held his breath and didn't move when the lass looked straight in his direction, certain she could hear the pounding of his heart. Once she crawled into the tent, Duncan hurried back to where his men remained.

"'Tis our group. The lass is sleeping in a tent about ten feet from where the warriors are camped, probably to give her privacy."

"Did ye see MacPherson?" John asked.

"Nay. mayhap he's following later. The bride might have requested time to settle in and get to ken the MacIntosh lad before the wedding. No matter to us. We will snatch her from her tent when everyone else is asleep."

"How do ye want to do this?" Kevin, another of his men asked.

"I will go with two others. We can access the lass from the back of the tent. We'll put a cloth over her mouth before we do anything else. Then drag her out and race back to the horses and head home. I'm counting on her being too shocked at being awakened in the middle of the night to make much noise."

"While we wait, we should eat something from our bags. Once we have the lass, we will ride straight through."

They'd brought oatcakes and blocks of cheese with them. They ate their food, passing around a flask of ale, and spoke softly, not wanting their voices to carry in the silence of the night.

As they ate and conversed, Duncan thought over their trip thus far. He was a tad surprised at how short a distance they had to travel to meet up with the group. 'Twould make it easier for them to escape and be behind the walls of their castle before anyone even knew where the lass had been taken, or who had taken her. Once they were legally married and he'd bedded the lass, he would make it known to the two clans that he had the bride.

Then he would prepare for battle, but with the MacPherson lass in his care and protection, he didn't believe 'twould result in much except a great deal of threats and insults. He would welcome his father-in-law, and they would have peace since he had no desire to ally himself with

MacPherson for the purpose of taking on the MacIntosh clan.

They wrapped up the leftovers of their food and settled down to wait. Duncan addressed the group. "We wait for a few more hours. John, ye go and watch the camp. Come back when the last mon has fallen asleep."

"They will have at least one mon standing watch," Kevin said.

"Aye. One of us will take him out, drag him off, and then we go for the lass."

'Twas growing cold, and they didn't dare light a fire. Being warriors, they were well used to dealing with cold, snow, and rain. A few of the men played a game with pebbles, now passing around the whisky to keep themselves warm.

Duncan remained busy thinking of all the issues he had left behind at the castle that he needed to deal with once they were back and his marriage had taken place.

Before he'd left, he'd spoken with Dennis Grant on the problems the man was having with his son, Brendan. 'Twas the laird they all turned to when they had a problem they couldna solve themselves. Duncan had offered the best advice he could to the man.

Send him to the lists to train to be a warrior. It sounded as though the lad had too much energy for farming, which is what his da, and his da before him, had done. With four other sons, Dennis could afford to lose one if it would bring peace to the household. Brendan should have arrived the next morn at the lists ready for his training. That should keep him out of trouble.

They waited about three hours before John returned. He squatted next to where Duncan sat, resting against a tree.

"All is quiet. There is one mon on duty, but things must have been easy for them so far because he doesn't look as wide awake as I would like one of us to be while on watch."

Duncan nodded. "Aye. But remember they are crossing from one clan's land to another's. They doona expect to run into much trouble, ye can tell that by the way they set up camp."

Duncan stood and waved at Daniel and Gregory. "Ye both come with me." He looked over at John. "The rest of ye be ready to ride the moment we return with the lass."

The men stood and followed Duncan, making their way quietly through the woods until they reached the outer part of the camp. Duncan signaled at Daniel to take out the guard.

He heard nothing, but after only a few minutes, Daniel was back at his side. "'Twas easy. The mon was asleep."

Duncan huffed. "'Tis lucky he dinna get his throat slit."

"Aye."

"We will go to the back of the tent," Duncan said. "Gregory, ye approach the lass from the back of the tent and cover her mouth with this cloth." He held out a strip of Grant plaid. "Daniel and I will pull her out and head back to the horses."

The men nodded. "Let's go."

Silently, and almost too easily, they reached the tent. With his dagger, Duncan slit the back of the tent. Gregory covered the lass's mouth with his hand, then quickly replaced it with the plaid they carried.

That apparently awakened her enough that she began kicking and rolling around. Before she could make any more noise, Duncan and Daniel grabbed her under her arms and pulled her out. She bucked and kicked, but

Duncan took her in his arms and tossed her over his shoulder.

Within minutes they were racing toward the horses, the lass bouncing on his shoulder and pounding on his back. He was worried her muffled cries might be heard, but so far, no one seemed to be coming after them.

At one point, she wiggled and almost threw herself to the ground, but he ignored it, merely grasping her tighter.

The men waiting for him were already mounted. He tossed the lass onto the horse, vaulted behind her on the animal, and they left the wooded area, quietly so as not to awaken the rest of her camp.

When they were far enough away, Duncan clamped the lass's hands together that she'd been using to slap and punch at him, then wrapped another piece of plaid around her hands.

Garbled words spewed from her mouth, but it only made him grin. He liked a spirited lass. This one would be good in the bedchamber. He had to hold tight to her, because more than once she tried to toss herself sideways.

Finally, he leaned down close to her ear. "Ye best behave yerself, lass. If ye throw yerself to the ground, ye may end up dead instead of married and carrying bairns."

She turned toward him, her eyes wide. "Muff noth mait?"

He assumed she was repeating his words. She would have plenty of time to speak once they were behind the castle walls. Now they needed to put as much distance between them and her escorts as they could.

They rode like the devil, not stopping until they reached the village close to Freuchie Castle. Outside of the Crow and the Cow public house, Duncan raised his arm, calling a halt to the group. He leaned down and spoke into the lass's ear. "Do ye need to relieve yerself, lass?"

She shoved her elbow so hard against his muscled stomach he almost felt it. She mumbled some words, then pitched her head back to hit him on his chin. He raised his hand again to the men. "We doona need to stop."

The group moved forward, and soon they were riding over the drawbridge and through the outer gates. "Close the gates and pull up the drawbridge," Duncan shouted as the last of the men rode through.

He jumped from his horse and pulled the MacPherson lass down. She immediately wacked him over the head with her bound hands, then stomped on his foot.

Knowing how angry the lass was, he had to hold in his laughter at her poor attempts to harm him. He was a warrior, had fought many battles, practiced his sword skills daily, and no hitting or stomping by this wee lass was going to hurt.

"Now, lass. I ken ye are upset, and for that I apologize."

She screamed something, her eyes flashing with anger. Her beautiful deep green eyes. Aye, the men who'd seen her at court were right. She was truly a bonnie lass. Pale skin just as they'd said, along with plush lips, and despite her slender size, curves in all the right places. He'd felt plenty of them as he held onto her during their ride.

"I'm going to remove yer bindings, lass, but be aware ye canna escape, so please doona try. I doona want ye to hurt yerself."

She glowered at him but remained still. First, he untied her hands, and when she didn't reach out to scratch his eyes out, he removed the cloth from her mouth.

He gave her a courtly bow. "Welcome to Freuchie Castle,

my lady. 'Twill be yer home from now on, once we are married."

The lass placed her hands on her hips and leaned forward. "I have no idea who ye are and why ye dragged me away from my group. Further, this place," she looked around, "'twill no' be my home, and we are no' marrying." Once more she stomped on his foot.

"Aye. I ken ye were expecting to marry up with the MacIntoshes, but I'm afraid we couldna allow that, so ye will marry me, instead."

"Ye lackwit. I'm not marrying anyone."

Allowing for the lass's anger at being taken, he didn't remind her she was speaking to the laird in a manner not acceptable. "Aye, lass. Ye are. Ye might be relieved that ye willna be wed to MacIntosh. From what I've heard, he's no' a nice mon, so ye are better off here."

Lady Agnes Pherson fisted her hands at her sides and growled. "I am better off back at my tent." She crossed her arms over her chest. "I demand ye return me right now."

He grinned, which probably only made her madder. "Now, Lady Agnes, ye need to settle yerself down."

Her arms dropped to her sides. "Who?"

He shook his head, smiling at her attempt at ignorance. "Lady Agnes MacPherson, daughter of Laird MacPherson."

She narrowed those beautiful eyes. "I have no idea of what ye are speaking, even though I understand the language. I am no' Lady Agnes whoever, I am Lady Elsbeth Johnstone, and I have no intention of marrying ye or anyone else since I am headed to a convent in Perth."

"Shite."

3

Elsbeth stared at the man who had just whisked her away from her group and then stood there claiming she was someone else. She wiped her palms down her face. "I canna believe this. Ye took the wrong lass."

"Aye." He shook his head. "But ye look just like her."

She stabbed his chest with her finger. "Nay. I look just like my twin sister, and she isna Lady Agnes whoever, either. Ach!" She turned and stomped away, not sure where she was going.

"Ye were headed to a convent?" His words seemed to be pulled from his chest.

"Aye."

"Have ye already taken yer vows?"

She turned back. "Nay."

He let out a deep sigh. "I doona ken what to say, lass. 'Tis sorry I am, but ye must believe the description we got of the lass we were looking for matches yers completely."

All this time, the men who had ridden with them stood

around, holding onto their horses, apparently not quite sure what to do.

She turned back. "And why were ye planning on taking that lass from her group?"

The laird looked a tad uneasy. "To marry."

"She is yer sweetheart, then?"

He shook his head, looking even more uncomfortable. "Nay. I've ne'er met her, which is the reason why we took ye by mistake."

Elsbeth crossed her arms over her chest and glared at him. "Are ye so verra poor in yer wooing skills that ye needed to steal a bride? No one else would have ye, then?"

He raised his chin, his shoulders straightening. "'Tis an alliance matter. Ye wouldna understand."

"Aye. I agree. I canna understand why a mon needs to pilfer someone else's betrothed."

'Twas early evening since they had ridden straight through to this castle from where she had been camping. She was exhausted and confused. How would she ever find her escort group again? Then she realized once they all woke up, they would find her missing. What would they do?

Probably look for her, and then return to Dornoch and tell her sister she was missing. Ach. What a mess!

She rubbed her eyes with the heels of her hands, trying very hard not to cry. She looked up at the man who seemed to be the leader of those who had taken her. He was no more than a few inches from her. She stepped back.

He held up his hand. "Please, Lady Elsbeth. I am truly sorry for the mistake we've made. I will be happy to escort you to yer convent."

"I doona even ken who ye are."

He offered a courtly bow. "My apologies. I am Laird Duncan Grant of Clan Grant."

"And what of my family? The men in my escort will look for me, and when they doona find me, they will return to my sister's keep, and she will be scared to death."

"Where is yer family? Isna Johnstone near the border?

"Aye. But I've been living with my sister and her husband, Laird Haydon Sutherland in Dornoch."

"Sutherland?" The man must have known Haydon because he started when Elsbeth mentioned his name.

"Aye."

"How far from where we found ye is Dornoch? I believe that is far up in the Highlands?"

"Aye. 'Twill take them a few days to look for me and then return home."

"I will send a missive to yer laird and tell him ye are under my protection and I will bring ye to the convent in Perth. I will make sure the messenger I send leaves immediately and rides straight through."

She felt dead on her feet. Little sleep, a strenuous trip thus far, and now this nonsense. When she began to sway a bit, the laird reached out and took her arm. "I believe ye need to have a hot bath, food, and then hours of sleep."

Elsbeth tried to look fierce, but she was afraid, in her condition, she looked more like an unkempt bairn looking for its mam. "I willna accept anything from ye until ye send someone to try to find my escort, and if no', then proceed to Dornoch and assure my sister all is well."

"Aye. If ye will follow me, ye can add a note to mine so yer sister can be comforted."

Thinking that Ainslee had not been comforted since Elsbeth had made her announcement about going to Perth, she doubted if this mishap would make her feel better. But since 'twas the only thing to be done, she might as well go along with the laird's plan. She nodded.

The laird turned and walked off, apparently expecting her to follow along like a puppy. But since there wasn't anything else to do, she did exactly that. He led her to a cozy room with a fire in the brazier. The room smelled of peat and whisky. She also picked up a light scent of the soap the laird must use since she'd noticed it when she was flush against him on the ride to the castle.

Despite her fear and annoyance, she'd also noticed the man's huge shoulders, muscular legs, and strong arms as he held her.

"Please have a seat, Lady Elsbeth." He waved to a chair in front of the large desk that took up a good portion of the room.

She sat and rearranged her skirts, attempting to keep herself awake long enough to get this finished. After their arrival at the castle, and she'd understood that the man didn't plan to harm her in any way, her fear dissolved, leaving her so exhausted she doubted any note she wrote to Ainslee would make any sense.

He drew out a piece of parchment, a sign that this was a wealthy clan. "What is yer sister's name?"

"Lady Ainslee Sutherland. She is married to Laird Haydon Sutherland."

He dipped his head. "So ye've said."

Elsbeth had always knew that Haydon was respected, and in some cases, even feared, among the other clans. His reputation had apparently made it to Clan Grant. While she wouldna say Laird Grant looked afraid of being involved with the Sutherlands, he certainly showed a great deal of respect for the man.

He dipped his quill in a small inkpot sitting on the desk. He stared into space for a moment, then began to write. The heat in the room and the comfort of the chair had Elsbeth growing sleepier by the minute. She had to force herself to keep from slumping face down on the desk in front of her.

Laird Grant blotted the parchment and looked up at her. "I've written that we mistakenly removed ye from yer escort, but since we are now aware of our mistake, I shall bring you, under my protection and with a suitable escort, to the convent in Perth."

Elsbeth nodded.

"Now if ye wish to write something in yer own hand that yer sister would recognize, we can have this missive sent off immediately." He slid the parchment across the desk. Elsbeth read it, not seeing anything that would alarm her sister unnecessarily. Laird Grant came across as penitent, protective, and ready to do the right thing.

After some consideration, Elsbeth merely wrote that everything the laird said was true. She was not being mistreated in any way and hoped to be on her way in another day or so. She also added she would send a missive the minute she arrived in Perth.

Why she was trusting the man with the words she'd written surprised her. So far, he didn't seem anything but contrite, but she prayed she wasn't making a huge mistake by reassuring her sister of her safety.

She pushed the message back across the desk. "I find myself exceedingly tired, Laird. If ye would be so kind as to have someone show me to a bed, I would be most grateful."

Hopefully, she didn't need to add to the laird that she

intended to sleep in said bed by herself. She was certainly not too tired to fight for her virtue if things didn't go the way he said they would.

He stood. "Of course, but I assume you would care for a bath and a meal before ye retire?"

"Aye. That would be most pleasant."

This time he walked to the door, then waved her in front of him. Since she didn't know where she was going, 'twould have been better had he done the same as before and had her follow him.

The laird stopped a young servant who was watching her with wide eyes. "Margaret, bring Lady Elsbeth to one of the guest bedchambers. Then please notify the chatelaine that we have a guest and to send up a bath and a hot meal for Lady Elsbeth. After that she is not to be disturbed until she makes her presence kenned."

The lass dipped a curtsey and looked at Elsbeth. "Please follow me, my lady, and I will show you to a comfortable room that is already prepared."

Once they arrived in the room that was as the young maid had said, quite comfortable, Elsbeth eyed the bed, but knew she would sleep much better if she were clean and her belly was full.

"My lady, I will have some of the men bring up the tub and water. In the meantime, I will request the meal from the kitchen and be back to help ye undress for the bath."

"Thank ye."

The lass looked her up and down. "I assume ye dinna have other clothes with ye?"

The anger at her predicament arose again. There was no reason to take it out on this young lass, though. "Nay. I can sleep in my chemise if ye can have someone brush off the road dust from my dress. That would be most appreciated."

"Of course, my lady. Just give me a moment to request what the laird had ordered, and I'll return soon."

* * *

Duncan gestured to the men who had ridden with him and now stood in the great hall, looking as though they wished to be anywhere else. "Into my solar."

Once they were all settled, a couple of the men in chairs, others leaning against the wall, Duncan began. "This is an utter mess."

No one disagreed.

"No' only did we abscond with the wrong lass, this one is headed to a convent." He ran his palm down his face. "As laird, I doona blame anyone but myself. Lady Elsbeth looks precisely like the description we were given. However, red curly hair and a bonnie face isna that unusual in the Highlands. Allowing that, we still made a huge error, and now no' only dinna we stop the wedding between the MacIntoshes and the MacPhersons, we have a lass in our custody who plans to serve the church."

He looked over at Daniel. "Pass the whisky."

His stomach had knotted when she said she was headed to a convent. A convent! Christ's toes, why would a lass who looks like Lady Elsbeth be headed to a convent? She should have been snapped up years ago and have a few bairns clutching her skirts.

Before she'd succumbed to exhaustion she'd certainly been spirited enough. There must be something wrong with the lads at Dornoch to let this beauty slip through their hands.

Ye need a bride.

Aye, was true, but a lass promised to the church? Although, she said she hadn't taken her vows yet. Then he upbraided himself. Instead of lusting after a lass headed to a convent, he should be thinking about the backlash he might be facing from The Sutherland.

"I believe we should step up our training."

"Are ye expecting trouble from her clan?" Gregory asked.

Duncan shrugged. "I doona ken. From what I ken of the Sutherland laird, he is a sensible one with a cool head on his shoulders, not one to instigate a war unless for a major insult."

Owen took a sip of whisky. "He just might consider his sister-by-marriage being taken from her escort a major insult."

"Aye," Duncan said.

They all sat in silence mulling over the mess they'd created, slowly finishing the jug of whisky. Finally, fed up with feeling sorry for himself for the mistake, Duncan slapped his thighs and stood. "'Tis time for bed. We canna do anything about the situation now. Best to eat and find our beds. Things might look better in the morn."

The only sound as the men stood and wandered toward the solar door was Owen's comment. "'Twill probably be raining in the morn."

THINGS DIDN'T LOOK BETTER in the morn, and Owen had been right. As Duncan looked out the window of his bedchamber, he could barely see the castle walls with the rain pouring down, as if crying for the lass who dwelt under his roof by mistake.

He washed and dressed for the day and headed to the great hall to break his fast. He stopped Margaret on his way down the stairs. "Do ye ken if Lady Elsbeth has arisen?"

"Aye, my laird. She's been up for a while and is right now finishing up her breakfast."

He nodded at the maid and continued to the great hall.

It appeared the lass was not one to lie in bed like a slug. Up and ready to go before he even made it downstairs. She was most likely anxious to be on her way, but he would have to break the news to her that with the weather as it was, they couldn't travel today, and depending on how much rain they saw, mayhap not for a couple days.

"Good morning, Lady Elsbeth," he said as he joined her at one of the lower tables. "Why are ye no' sitting on the dais? As a guest, ye should be seated there."

The lass glared at him. "I am no' a guest. I am a captive. A prisoner."

He smiled, trying to improve her mood before he gave her the bad news about not being able to travel today. "Nay. Ye are no' a prisoner. Again, I must apologize for the error we made."

She just closed her eyes and shook her head, then continued with her bowl of porridge.

"Did ye sleep well?"

"Aye." She barely got the word out.

"The bed was comfortable?"

She turned on him, her beautiful eyes flashing. "Aye, Laird. Everything was wonderful. The bath hot, the food well cooked, and the bed comfortable. Yer chatelaine, Bridget, was verra helpful and kind. The only problem is I shouldna' be here to experience all those pleasures."

He wished she hadn't mentioned pleasures since watching her fiery spirit only made him think of other pleasures they could share.

She's going to be a nun.

One of the serving maids placed a trencher in front of him, along with a platter of sausage, eggs, brown bread, and tomatoes. He filled the trencher and tried again to be sociable. "Ye seem a tad old to be going to a convent."

As soon as the idiotic words left his mouth, he wished them back. As expected, the lass glared again. "I wanted to make sure I arrived before my dotage set in, Laird." She clipped the last few words through clenched teeth.

Mayhap, he was better off just eating his meal and moving on with his day. Just as he'd convinced himself that was the best decision, she turned to him. "What time do we leave?"

God's bones. Either she hadn't looked out the windows, or she was unfamiliar with travel. "Ah, lass, I doona think we can leave today."

She reared back as if slapped. "Why no'?"

"The rain. All the waterways will be flooding, making it much too dangerous to travel. We need to wait until the rain stops and then assess what the roads look like."

Her beautiful, plump lips were pursed, and her face turned red. "Ye are afraid of a little water?"

He made another mistake and laughed. Based on her scowl, not a good idea. "Lass, be reasonable. I'm thinking of yer safety. I promised yer laird that I would see ye safely to the convent in Perth. I would be remiss in my duty and promise to him if we set out today. I'm afraid ye are stuck here for a day and possibly two."

After staring at him for a few moments, her shoulders slumped in acceptance, and he breathed a sigh of relief. Was she so anxious then to enter a convent?

She propped her chin up on her hand, her elbow resting on the table. "I'm afraid I am no' one to sit around all day, Laird. If I'm no' to be allowed to leave today, then I need something to do."

"Ye are a guest! Ye needn't work."

"Nay. A prisoner."

"A guest." His voice grew louder.

"A prisoner," she shouted back.

'Twas then he noticed they had gathered the interest of the others in the hall. He lowered his voice. Mayhap it would improve the lass's mood if she had something to do besides fret about the weather and her convent. "What were yer duties at the Sutherland keep?"

She narrowed her eyes. "Why?"

"Does everything I say cause suspicion?"

"Aye. I'm here where I have no reason to be instead of on my way to Perth. Ye say I'm a guest, no' a prisoner, but if I tried to leave, I ken ye would stop me."

"Of course." He ran his fingers through his hair. "I canna let ye leave without an escort, and we can't travel in this weather."

She crossed her arms over her chest. "So, I am a prisoner."

"Look, lass, I just want to ken what ye did at Dornoch."

She shrugged. "A few different things. I took care of the garden, helped in the kitchen when they were busy, and trained under the clan healer."

"Well, if ye doona mind, our healer is getting up in years, and I ken she could use some help while ye are here. Especially with the herbs she mixes for her patients."

The lass's eyes lit up, and once more he had to mentally shake his head at this beautiful lass locking herself away in a convent.

"I can help with that. Working with the herbs was the part of the job I enjoyed the most because of my love of gardening." She paused for a moment. "Will she mind if I took on a few duties while I'm stuck here?"

He smiled. "Ye are no' stuck here, lass." He held his hand up when she opened her mouth to speak. "And nay ye are not a prisoner, we are merely waiting for the weather to clear so we can escort ye to Perth."

She offered him the first smile since he'd dragged her out of her tent. His man bits came alive, and he had to quell his thoughts if he were to stand and show her to Madeline's room where she did her healing.

He finished his breakfast while thinking about snakes, puppies, mud holes, and old grouchy Gillis with the wart on her nose and her remaining teeth brown as dirt. That did the trick, and as soon as he swallowed the last of his ale, he was able to stand and escort Lady Elsbeth to Madeline's room with dignity.

4

*E*lsbeth found that the healer, Madeline, was both pleasant and quite intelligent. She was an older woman but hadn't lost any of her wits. She was more than happy to have Elsbeth help her while she was stuck in the castle.

Madeline had been given a room in the keep on the bottom floor that had been set aside for her use, unlike Dorathia who'd had a small cottage inside the outer bailey at Dornoch.

Once the laird had introduced her and left, Madeline studied Elsbeth for a few moments. "Can I ask ye, lass, how ye come to be here if ye are part of the Sutherland clan?"

Elsbeth smiled at the healer. "I'm not part of the Sutherland Clan, actually. I am from the Johnstone Clan, and was living with my sister and her husband, the Laird of Sutherland. I was on my way to join a convent in Perth when I was…" She wasn't quite sure how to describe her situation to this lovely woman. Honesty was probably the best thing. "I was taken from my escort group and brought here."

The woman's brows rose. "Indeed? And why was that?"

"'Twas a mistake. The laird and his men thought I was someone else."

Her eyes twinkled, a sly smile on her wrinkled face. "Ach. So now ye will stay here. Marry the laird?"

"Nay!" Both shock and something unfamiliar raced through her body. "I am waiting for the weather to clear, and then I will be on my way to the convent."

Madeline nudged Elsbeth in the ribs. "The laird is a braw mon, verra handsome and caring. He'd make ye a fine husband. Between the two of ye, ye'd have strong and beautiful bairns."

Why did the entire world think she should marry? Why did they fail to respect the decision she'd made that concerned her life? Mayhap she didn't ever want to marry.

Liar.

Even if she did, no man had ever made her feel the way her sister felt about her husband. Just because Laird Grant had caused shivers when he touched her meant nothing. The man had taken her prisoner. She wouldna give him another thought.

"Nay. I have my mind made up. 'Tis to serve the Lord."

"Ah, lass." She reached her aged hand out and touched Elsbeth's forehead. A strange feeling settled over her. "The Lord works in strange ways, my lady. There might be a reason why ye were taken by mistake." She winked.

"Aye. I was taken by mistake because I apparently look like the lass Laird Grant was trying to capture and force to marry him. 'Tis no' the sort of mon I would be looking with favor upon."

Instead of arguing, the old woman merely smiled and

nodded at her. "Since ye are here for a bit of time, let me tell ye what ye can do to help the most."

Comfortable once again with no more talk of the laird, and ready to discuss what she could do to help this woman with her healing, Elsbeth eagerly watched and listened as Madeline pointed out the various bowls of herbs and explained which plants needed to be crushed and mixed with others. 'Twas familiar work for Elsbeth, and she was glad to have something to occupy her time until she could leave.

And to keep her out of Laird Grant's way.

She didn't care for the way he looked at her. Nor how she felt when he accidentally, or mayhap not by accident, touched her. Her heart fluttered, and her stomach gave host to a cluster of butterflies.

The two women enjoyed a comfortable and productive morning. Elsbeth was amazed at how quickly the time passed. Although she'd helped Dorathia at the Sutherland clan, she was but an extra person there as well as everywhere else in Dornoch castle since Dorathia was training her niece Helen to take her place when she grew too old to work.

Madeline stepped back from the table where they had been working and smiled. "Thanks for yer help, lass. 'Twould have taken me three days to do all ye did in one morning." She tapped her hip. "These old bones doona work as well as they used to."

"I was more than happy to help." In fact, she felt more useful than she had in a very long time.

Just then a knock on the door to Madeline's room drew their attention. A man who had been in the group that had taken her from her escort group stood at the threshold. He pulled his cap off and gave her a slight bow. "My lady, the laird has requested that I escort ye to the great hall for the nooning."

Her stomach rumbled, reminding her that she was indeed hungry. She turned to Madeline. "Will ye be joining us, then?"

"Nay. I take my meals in the kitchen." She gave Elsbeth a shove. "But ye are a guest, so ye should be in the great hall."

"I'm a prisoner," she mumbled as she sailed through the door, not waiting for the man who'd fetched her to escort her. She certainly knew where the great hall was. She wasn't helpless.

After wandering the halls of the keep, she finally asked one of the serving maids where the great hall was. The lass brought her there, not very far from where she first entered the keep. When she spotted the man who had been sent for her, she hoped her face didn't flush red.

It did.

"Where were ye, lass?" The laird asked.

"I, um, had something else to do first." She turned an even brighter red when she realized what that must have sounded like.

He ignored her discomfort, and she took the seat next to him that he waved at. She didn't want to sit on the dais with him and the other men. She wasn't a guest.

"I should have introduced ye to my men."

Before Elsbeth told him she had no need to know the men who had taken her, Duncan continued. He pointed to the man on the other side of him. "Owen, my second-in-command." He then went down the row." John, Kevin, Danie, and Gregory. All of them Grants." Each man nodded as his name was spoken.

She offered a partial smile. She didn't want to be rude, but really, why would she want to ken the names of the men who had dragged her away from her escort group?

Laird Grant began to fill the trencher in front of her with food from the platters on the table in front of them. The nooning at Dornoch wasn't as formal as this one. Most times the warriors would wander in during a break in training and grab a meal. The family sometimes made use of the great hall, and other times they had food sent to Haydon's solar where the laird, Ainslee, Maura, and Conall would eat together, bouncing their bairns on their knees.

Feeling uncomfortable, and like an extra leg on a horse, she'd stopped joining them a few months before. Most times she would sit in the kitchen and grab something light before she returned to the garden. The afternoon was her favorite time to be out in the fresh air.

"How was yer morning with Madeline?" The larid asked as he broke a bannoch in half, handing her a piece.

She intended to ignore his attempt at social discourse, still smarting at her predicament, but her years of training in good manners wouldna allow her to do that. "'Twas fine."

He continued to study her until she added with a huff. "Madeline is a verra bright woman. I learned a lot from our healer, Dorathia, but Madeline had some herbs I've ne'er heard about."

The laird gave a curt nod. "I'm sure she appreciated yer help."

"Aye. She said so." After about two more bites of stew, she asked, "Can we leave tomorrow, Laird?"

He shook his head. "I take it ye have no' been out of the keep? 'Tis still raining, and quite heavily at that. Even if the rain stops today, I canna see us leaving for another few days."

He poured more ale into his cup and hers. "Why are ye so anxious to leave? Ye canna wait to lock yerself away from the world?

She bristled, once again annoyed at being questioned about her decisions. "'Tis a promise I made to Sister Albert, Laird. She is expecting me, and I doona like to disappoint anyone. Ye see, I am an honorable woman. I keep my word."

Instead of frowning at her, the laird laughed, irritating her further. She refused to be moved by his handsome face when he laughed. His black hair, hazel eyes, and short beard that he must have thought covered the scar on his cheek, did strange things to her middle. Again.

Her chin moved up a notch. "What is so humorous, Laird?"

"Ah, lass. First of all, I wish ye would call me Duncan. Next, I ken ye are trying to explain yerself and insult me at the same time. I agree, whisking away a lass on her way to her wedding doesn't sound honorable."

He raised his hand as she started to speak. "But there are times when ye must do what ye think is best for yer clan. As laird, I am responsible for the safety and well-being of everyone in Clan Grant. With an alliance between the two clans on either side of us, we are no' as safe as we were last month."

"But ye dinna stop the wedding, since ye took the wrong lass."

He winced. "Aye. A mistake I'm afraid might cost us in the future."

How could she possibly feel sorry for the man? He tried to steal a woman away from her intended husband. Of course, with how things were done most times, the MacPherson lass probably had no say in marrying the MacIntosh son.

"What is the mon like that Lady Agnes MacPherson is to marry?"

The Laird—she wasn't able to think of him as Duncan—leaned back in his chair. "From what we've heard, not a nice one. I actually felt as though I was saving the lass from an unpleasant life."

Now 'twas Elsbeth's turn to laugh. "It sounds to me as if ye are looking for a reason to excuse yer behavior."

He grinned back, and they stared at each other for a few moments, their smiles fading. Elsbeth pulled her eyes away and stared at her meal. She knew her cheeks were red, and why she didn't know.

Yes, ye do, lassie.

* * *

DUNCAN WAS MORE ENCHANTED every minute by this lass who was determined to enter a convent. He'd tried all morning to forget about her but kept going over in his mind the lass's smile, the way she tilted her chin up, and the fire in her eyes when she was angry. At him, generally.

He'd never spent a great deal of time thinking about taking a wife. Due to being laird, he knew it was something he needed to do. At eight and twenty, he knew it would be soon but had no interest in any of the lasses he'd met at Court.

Like every laird, he would be looking for a wife who would bring a strong alliance with her. He had to admit, if only to himself, the idea of kidnapping the MacPherson lass had held appeal because he wouldna have to go through the search for a wife and all that it involved. A bride who would bring a strong alliance to his clan.

Lady Elsbeth Johnstone was even more suitable than any other lass he could think of. Related to the powerful Sutherland clan high up in the Highlands by marriage, and the solid Johnstone clan, who were thought well of, near the border by birth, she had all the requirements for a fitting bride for him.

In addition to her formidable connections, she was a beautiful lass, pleasant—at least when not scowling at him—and possessed a body that any man would be pleased to see in his bed. Like all lairds' daughters, she'd also been raised to manage a keep.

She was perfect. And unattainable.

"May I ask ye for something, Laird?" Elsbeth placed her eating dagger on the table alongside her trencher.

"Aye. But no' to leave before the roads clear. That I canna offer ye. But to grant yer request, I require ye address me as Duncan."

She nodded. "Do ye have books?"

The lass continued to surprise him. He didn't know of any lass in the castle, or for that matter at court, who would ask about books. He knew she could read because she'd written a note to her sister, but to inquire about books was not something anyone had ever asked him. "I have books in my solar. Do ye enjoy reading?"

"Aye. My da made sure my sister and I could read and do our numbers. He had several books in our keep, but I read them all. Laird Sutherland keeps some books as well, but again, I read all of them. I'm always looking for something new."

Duncan pushed his chair back. "Come with me, lass, and we'll see if the books I have are new to ye."

She beamed, and his heart gave an extra thump. Why did this lass appeal to him so very much? 'Twas not just her looks, either. Aye, she would be a perfect wife for him, but she also had something special that made him feel more than what he'd thought taking a wife would bring.

He sighed with the way his mind had been distracted since they pulled the lass out of her tent. If she was determined to enter the convent in Perth, then he needed to get his mind far away from where it had been wandering.

The solar was quiet as usual. He spent his time there going over the ledgers and notes about the production of the various farms and crofters. On a regular basis, he met with various clan members and tenants who had problems that they brought to their laird.

Then there were also the times when he held court there and made decisions on numerous situations and problems. Another reason he would love to have a wife was to share some of the burden with him. A woman was needed in difficult dealings, and he was always at a loss when something turned up that needed a gentler hand.

"My goodness. Ye do have quite a bit of books." She spun in a circle taking in all the shelves. She looked over her shoulder at him after pulling a book from the shelf. "Do ye read too, Laird?"

"Duncan," he said as he walked over to where she stood. "I asked ye to call me Duncan. Is that so hard for ye, lass?"

Once again, spots of red appeared on her cheeks. That seemed to happen a lot around him. Was it possible a lass promised to the church could have the same strange feelings toward him as he did towards her?

He reached out and touched her chin. Skin so soft, a faint smell of flowers drifting toward his nose. "What say ye?"

She shook her head. "I dinna see any reason to call ye by yer name. I'll be here a short time and then off to the convent. It doesn't matter what I call ye."

His fingertip traced her plush lips, then wandered to her throat until his thumb and forefinger cupped her chin. He could see the pounding of the vein in her neck. Aye, she was affected.

Before he could give it any more thought, he slowly bent his head, giving her the opportunity to push him away. She studied him with wide eyes but didn't move. He brushed a gentle kiss to her moist, warm lips. Back and forth he went, and once encouraged, he wrapped his arms around her waist and pulled her against him.

She whimpered but didn't push him away. He angled his head so he could take the kiss deeper. She gasped as he touched her lips with his tongue, allowing him to sweep into the damp heat of her mouth. She tasted of the honey on the bannoch and the bitterness of the ale.

If there was anything such as a perfect kiss, this was it. Just as he was settling in for a lengthy exploration of her mouth, her hands edged up between their bodies, and she pushed against his chest.

"Nay."

He released her, never one to force himself on a lass. She was panting as was he. Closing his eyes, he shook his head. "I'm sorry, lass. I ne'er should have done that."

"Nay," her lips uttered, but her eyes said something different. "Do I need to be concerned for my safety here after all?" The words barely made it past her lips with her gasping for air.

He straightened up, almost shocked at what he'd done. And how perfect it had seemed. "No need, Elsbeth. I shall ne'er do that again. 'Tis no' my habit to take advantage of a woman under my protection." He offered her a slight bow and left the room before he changed his mind and did the very thing he just claimed he would never do.

A good long battle on the lists was exactly what he needed. He glanced out the door of the great hall as one of his warriors came inside, shaking himself like a wet dog.

Christ's toes. Would it never stop raining?

5

Elsbeth touched her fingers to her lips. The place where the laird—Duncan—had set his lips. She never felt anything like it. As most young women, she'd had a few slight brushes over her lips from a man or two in her youth, but nothing like what just happened.

She understood a bit more now why Maura and Ainslee smiled so much. If that was the beginning of what happened in the bedchamber between husband and wife, it explained a lot, and exposed her ignorance about such things.

She chastised her silliness and headed for the door to the solar, following Duncan out. Her life was at the convent. 'Twas a decision she'd made, and she would stand by it. In fact, 'twas the first decision she'd made by herself *for herself* in her entire life. Always she'd followed Ainslee's ideas and direction from the time they'd been bairns in the nursery.

A dark cloud of doubt passed over her. Had she made a mistake the very first time she tried to run her own life?

With all her musing, it wasn't until she reached her

bedchamber that she realized she hadn't taken a book with her, so distracted she'd been with Duncan's kiss.

Gracious. She'd thought of him by his given name. Not that anything would come of that.

Pulling back the fur cover over the window in her bedchamber, she looked glumly at the pouring rain. She needed the rain to stop and the roads to clear so she could leave for Perth. She feared the more time she spent with the laird of Clan Grant, the more danger she placed herself in, and she wasn't thinking about him harming her. Not in a way that would hurt. Physically, at least.

Staring at the downpour, she went over in her mind the kiss they'd shared. At first, she had been startled and then she realized he'd managed to stir something inside her. The place in her stomach where the butterflies had gathered before had become as lively as a Scottish reel.

Just thinking of it had her heart thumping again. She'd also heard his heart pounding away against her breasts when he pulled her close. Whatever it had been that she'd felt, it seemed she was not alone in her reaction.

Torn between searching for the laird and asking him to do it again or finding a quiet corner where she could pray and remind herself where she was headed spurred her to leave her bedchamber. Aye, prayer was the best decision. Pray for strength to avoid Duncan and for the blasted rain to stop so she could leave.

She found a quiet corner, but shamefully was soon bored. She got up off her knees, rubbed the joints, and headed to the kitchen. She knew from her years at both the Johnstone and Sutherland keeps that kitchen help was always needed.

"Good afternoon, my lady." The smiling rotund woman

TO YIELD TO A HIGHLANDER

who appeared to be in charge of the kitchen greeted her from where she stood with two scullery maids, giving them instructions. "I understand ye are staying with us for a while."

Word certainly traveled fast in a keep. "Aye. I'm on my way to a convent in Perth. I'm just waiting for the rain to cease so the laird can escort me there."

The cook's brows rose. "A convent? Why would a lass such as yerself be headed to a convent?"

It took quite a bit of control to tamp down her annoyance. She was very tired of everyone being surprised by her decision. Instead, she smiled. "'Tis what I want. Now though, I had hoped to help ye in the kitchen, so I have something to do to pass the time here. I doona believe I ken yer name."

Obviously taken aback at her abrupt manner, the cook hesitated, then said, "My name is Beatrice Grant." She shook her head. "But I'm afraid I canna allow ye to work in the kitchen, my lady. The laird would no' be pleased. Ye are a guest."

Ach. If she heard that phrase one more time she would scream. She wasn't a guest. She was a prisoner. A guest received an invitation and decided if she wanted to accept. A guest was not dragged from her sleep, tossed over a horse, and then hauled into a keep and told she had to stay there.

Trying to be as sweet as her nature generally was, she smiled at the cook once again. "I believe the laird would be fine with me working in the kitchen. I helped yer healer, Madeline, this morning." She quickly added, "With his blessing."

The entire time Elsbeth spoke, the cook continued to

shake her head. "Kitchen help is much more difficult. Messy and dirty. I canna allow that."

Gritting her teeth, Elsbeth nodded. "Thank ye for yer concern, Beatrice." With those terse words she turned on her heel and strode down the corridor to the great hall.

After pacing in the large empty area, and against her better judgment, she once more sought Duncan's solar. Despite needing to stay away from him for her own personal sanity, she was faced with losing her sanity if she didn't find a way to keep herself busy. She was not used to sitting about, playing the lady.

If she were lucky, he would be off somewhere, and she could search his books for something to read in peace.

It appeared her luck this day was lacking. After she knocked, a soft, 'come,' had her taking a deep breath and opening the door. Duncan was there, but she breathed a sigh of relief when she saw Owen sitting in the chair in front of the laird's desk.

"Excuse me, Laird, but I ne'er did get the book. If I am not interrupting, may I search for one?"

Her heart thumped and her stomach clenched at the look on his face. His countenance brightened, and he smiled. Even Owen noticed as he grinned at the two of them. She scowled. The last thing she needed was another person in the keep edging her toward the laird.

"Aye, please help yerself, Elsbeth."

So, he was using her given name. No more 'my lady.' Well, she might think of him as Duncan, but she wouldna give in and address him so. "Thank ye."

She wandered back to the bookshelves, pulling out a book, flipping through the pages, and putting it back again. Most of the tomes were historical accounts of Clan Grant.

There was one entitled *Mr. William Shakespeare's Comedies, Histories & Tragedies.*

'Twas a very lengthy book, comprised of numerous pages with six and thirty plays. 'Twould keep her busy for a long time. She had enjoyed reading some of Mr. Shakespeare's plays before and looked forward to passing the time while she waited to leave.

"'That's quite a heavy book, Elsbeth. Do ye need help in carrying it?" Duncan's smooth, deep voice rolled over her. She turned to see that while she'd been busy browsing for a book, Owen had taken his leave.

Not good.

The laird leaned back in his chair, studying her with more intensity than she was comfortable with.

"Nay, Laird. I believe I can make it up to my bedchamber without help." She lifted the hefty book and headed to the door.

He jumped up, and before she even knew it, he stood in front of her holding the door open.

She nodded. "Thank ye."

"Elsbeth."

She stopped, her forehead pinched. "Aye?"

"Do ye play chess?"

She smiled. "Aye. I love a good game of chess. Do ye play?"

"I do. I was thinking perhaps after supper this evening we could play a few games."

"I would like that, Laird."

He reached out and touched her hand. "I would like ye to call me Duncan. I also wish to apologize again for kissing ye. I just doona want ye to feel uneasy around me."

Why did the man have to be so nice? He'd kidnapped

her. She had to remember that. She was not here by invitation, but by force.

Except he'd been nothing but remorseful and kind since he learned of his mistake. God's bones she was always so confused when she was around this man.

"I will try to remember to call ye Duncan, but since we will part ways in a couple of weeks, it doesn't seem like something for ye to fret about."

The laird burst out laughing and leaned his forearm against the doorjamb, getting entirely too close to her. "I'm a warrior, lass, and laird of Clan Grant. I doona fret. That's for lasses."

Her breathing began to speed up. She needed to get away, or she would find herself in his arms again, playing with the soft hair that curled over the back of his leine. Unlike other men, he didn't wear his hair long and pulled back with a piece of leather. 'Twas shorter, which seemed to suit him better.

She backed away. "If ye will excuse me, Laird—Duncan—I will make good use of this book." Before he could even answer her, she raced away, up the stairs, arriving at her bedchamber out of breath and flushed.

* * *

DUNCAN SAT ON THE DAIS, chatting with Owen and Gregory. As much as he attempted not to do it, his eyes kept wandering to the corridor where Elsbeth would appear for the evening supper.

The rain had finally stopped, and he'd sent one of his men out to assess the roads. As expected, when the man returned, he confirmed they were flooded. In the man's estimation, as long as the rain didn't start up again, they should be able to travel in two days.

'Twould be good to get Elsbeth out of the keep and into the convent she so desired. Except he wasn't sure that's what the lass really wanted. He knew she didn't like to be questioned about it, but it made him wonder if the reason was that she wasn't so sure herself.

Just then, she entered the great hall and headed in his direction. His stomach muscles clenched at the sight of her. One of the maids had gone through a trunk of dresses left behind by one of his mother's guests a few years before. They were most likely outdated as far as fashion was concerned for a genteel lady, but they fit her well and she looked wonderful in the deep blue dress that accented her curves.

A finer lass had never graced the room. She was beautiful, but aside from that, she was gracious and charming. She smiled at a few of the clansfolk as she made her way across the room. Apparently, in the short time she'd been at the keep, she'd already made some acquaintances.

It annoyed him to no end when she stopped to speak with one of the warriors who watched her like she was his next meal. If she didn't move on soon, he would be forced to jump over the table and pummel the lad.

"Yer drooling, Laird."

Duncan whipped his head around to see Owen staring at him with a huge grin on his face.

"I am no' drooling. Doona be ridiculous." He picked up his cup of ale and took a swallow, pretending to ignore Elsbeth, but watching her over the rim of his cup.

Finally, the lass joined them at the table. He stood and

pulled out the chair next to him. "Ye look beautiful, my lady."

"Thank ye." She settled in, and he waved at a serving maid. "Please bring her ladyship a cup of ale." He looked at Elsbeth. "Or do ye prefer wine?"

"Actually, I would prefer wine. Thank ye."

He tapped his fingertip on the table, suddenly uncomfortable. The lass did that to him. What he wanted to say and what he could say were widely different. He wanted to ask her to give up the idea of a convent and marry him.

Aye. That was precisely what he wanted to say. She would be perfect, and not just because a match with her would be beneficial to the clan or save him from a search. In the beginning, those had been his considerations.

Since then, he'd realized there were other reasons he would like to see Elsbeth as his wife.

"Did ye get far along in yer book?" he asked.

Elsbeth placed her hand over her mouth and tried to hide a giggle. "In truth, I began to read and grew sleepy. I took a nice, restorative nap and dinna get far with Mr. Shakespeare."

Duncan laughed. The lass had a sense of humor, which was one more reason he would enjoy life with her. "'Tis a good thing ye napped because ye will be wide awake for our chess game."

"Ah, Laird, I'm certain I can beat ye while half asleep."

His brows rose, and he took a sip of ale. "Is that so? I doona ken about that, lass. I'm as fierce on the chessboard as I am on a battlefield."

She nodded her thanks to the lass who put the cup of wine in front of her. "Ye should not say that, Laird. 'Twill only make me concentrate all the more."

He leaned in close to her. "Duncan."

Her cheeks flushed, and she cast her eyes in the other direction.

Duncan sat back and pondered his guest. Why he continued to flirt with the lass and insist upon her using his given name was just as confusing to him as the feelings she aroused in him.

"I see that the rain has stopped. Do ye have any idea when we can leave for Perth?" The softness of her voice stirred him in places he shouldna be thinking of.

"Ah. So anxious ye are to leave us? Have we no' been hospitable enough for ye?" He attempted to put humor into his words, but the undertone of bewilderment was clear to his ears.

"Hospitality doesn't play a part when ye are held prisoner."

He hated how her words stabbed at his heart. No matter how pleasant he was, how much he tried to offer comfort and ease to her visit, she was adamant about being a prisoner. Mayhap, he should throw her in the unused-for-years dungeon so she could feel what being a prisoner was truly like.

"Doona throw me in the dungeon, please," she said, her eyes dancing with mirth.

He started. "Did I say that out loud?"

She grinned. "Aye."

"Ach. I have a habit of doing that."

"Best no' do that when we play chess. Ye will then tell me the only reason I beat ye so roundly was because ye told me yer moves."

The food arrived on large platters placed on the tables. The serving lasses had added trenchers in front of them.

Using his good manners, Duncan placed the best pieces of meat and vegetables in Elsbeth's trencher. She nodded her thanks and drew her eating dagger from her belt.

Owen caught his attention, and they discussed various issues with the clan and the possibility of some rancor due to the alliance between the MacPhersons and the MacIntoshes.

His second-in-command lowered his voice and leaned in close to Duncan's ear. "Have ye thought about the advantages to Clan Grant if ye were to talk the bonnie lass next to ye into marriage instead of the convent? Sutherland and Johnstone would make for a verra strong alliance." He gave him a wink.

"The lady has her mind set on a convent."

Owen waved his hand. "Pfft. She doona ken what she wants. I'm willing to wager the lass is suffering a broken heart and her solution is to run away." He leaned even farther down. "There's more than one way to trap a rabbit, ye ken."

"Doona be silly. Her ladyship already feels like she's a prisoner. If I were to even give thought to talking her out of her plans, the last thing that would work with her is any sort of entrapment."

Owen shrugged and picked up his cup. "Then use yer mighty skills with the lasses."

Duncan slumped in his chair, fingering the ale cup. Mighty skill with the lasses? The man must be mad. Certainly, he'd had enough success over the years where bedsport was concerned, but he'd hardly consider himself a libertine.

He glanced over at Elsbeth who was in the middle of a lively conversation with Daniel, seated on her other side.

So, Owen believed the lass was running from a broken heart? He'd be a cad to take advantage of that.

Then again, no sacrifice was too great for a laird to make for his clan. When the conversation between Daniel and Elsbeth came to an end, he placed his hand on hers and gave it a slight squeeze. "'Tis time for our chess game, my lady. Are ye ready to lose?"

6

Elsbeth walked alongside Duncan as they made their way from the great hall. She'd been able to control her strangely uncomfortable feelings when near Duncan at dinner with everyone else in the room and during her conversation with one of his men.

Now 'twould be only the two of them. And a chess board.

He led her to a room she'd not been to before. He opened the door and waved her inside. Everything about the room spoke of a man's domain. Comfortable but large masculine furniture filled the spaces. Directly across from the fireplace, a dresser took up quite a bit of space on one wall. Several glass drinking vessels and a jug sat there.

Duncan placed his hands on his hips and looked around. "'Tis my quiet room. At least that is what I call it. When things get too loud and annoying, I retreat here."

"Ah. But when things get too loud and annoying, ye do no' fret, though?" She smiled, and he joined her with his own grin.

"Aye."

She wandered the room a bit, feeling the presence of a powerful man. In the corner sat a small table with two chairs and a chess board already set up. "Do ye play as yer own partner?"

"Aye," he said. "I doona invite many people into this room, and I find playing both sides of the chessboard verra relaxing."

"Indeed? I ne'er thought about doing that. To me it sounds confusing, but I must try it sometime."

She wasn't sure if she should be flattered or worried that he invited so few people into his domain, not sure if she wanted that honor and what it meant. He pointed toward the small table. "Since ye will have a partner tonight, ye won't have to struggle with that now." He pulled out a chair and she sat. She picked up the queen on her side of the board, turning to study the details. "These pieces are beautiful."

"Thank ye. I carved them myself." The pride was evident in his voice.

She put down the queen and picked up a bishop. "Ye are full of surprises, Laird."

"Duncan, please." He rubbed his hands together. "Are ye ready, lass?"

"Aye." Since the chair he'd pulled out for her faced the lighter pieces, 'twas her turn to begin the game. She studied the board for a moment, then used her usual opening, e4.

"Ah, going to play cautiously," Duncan said. He reached out and countered with e5.

"And ye are doing the same," she said as she continued with Nf3.

Duncan's long fingers hesitated for a moment, then did what she'd expected him to do. Nc6.

And so, the game continued. At first, she did everything as usual when she played the game, but Duncan was more of a challenge than anyone she'd played with in a long time. 'Twas good because she had to keep her mind on the chessboard which meant she wasn't thinking about the man sitting across from her.

His large presence was overwhelming if she allowed herself to think about it. His broad shoulders and muscled forearms looked almost absurd as he picked up a chess piece and moved it. No man as formidable as the laird should look so comfortable playing a game of chess.

'Twas another reason for her conflicting feelings. Although a brawny laird and warrior, he had his softer side, which is the one that troubled her the most. 'Twould be easy to dismiss him if he only showed the rough part of himself.

"Check." Elsbeth said with a grin.

Two more moves and Duncan returned her smile and slid his bishop. "Checkmate."

"Oh no, I dinna see that coming." She leaned back in her chair, annoyed at herself for allowing her musings to distract her. "'Twas a good game, Duncan."

His eyes grew warm at the use of his given name. "Ye are a good player, Elsbeth. Better than I had given ye credit for. 'Tis not too many lasses that can compete in the game."

They began to reset the board. "My sister didn't have the patience to sit and play the game, so I wandered the keep from the time I was about ten years to find someone to play with me," Elsbeth said as she moved her pieces into the proper spaces. "I think playing with so many others with different ideas on how to win the game helped me to learn and grow."

She made her first move. "What of yer family? I assume ye were an only child?"

"Aye. My mam died giving birth to my sister." He paused as he studied the board. "That was about twelve years ago. From the time we kenned she was expecting again, her health wasn't good. She'd already lost a few bairns, and she was older with this last one." He shook his head. "The bairn dinna make it, either."

"How verra sad. 'Twas just ye and yer da then?" Another good move gave her one of his bishops.

"Aye. But he ne'er recovered from her death. He was besotted with her," he grinned, then frowned, wiping the smile from his face. "I think his love for her is what took his life."

Elsbeth sucked in a breath, the pawn she planned to move fisted in her hand. "Why would ye say that?"

"He died on the battlefield about a year after my mam passed. I've always thought his skills had diminished because he just dinna have the will to live anymore."

There wasn't much she could say to comfort him that wouldna sound insipid. They continued to play in silence for a few minutes. "Ye were young when ye became laird, then?"

"Aye." Duncan reached out and moved another piece. "I was barely seventeen summers. Thankfully, my da had set up a group of advisors in case he should unexpectedly leave me with the running of the clan at a young age."

Elsbeth wondered if planning for that possibility was another reason why the laird thought his father's death was due to the sorrow he'd felt at the passing of his wife.

"From what I've seen while I've been here, it appears ye've done a good job." She moved her knight into place. "Check."

Duncan leaned his elbow on the table, his chin resting on his fist as he studied the board. "Verra good, my lady. I doona see a way out of this, either."

Elsbeth sat back and grinned. "One round to ye, and one to me."

'Twas probably growing late, but this was the most entertaining time she'd had since she'd been brought to the keep. They re-set the board again. Duncan looked up at her. "Would ye care for a drink?"

She scrunched up her nose. "I canna take ale this late in the evening. It plays havoc with my stomach."

He pushed his chair back and stood. "How about some fine Scottish whisky?"

"I ne'er had hard spirits."

"Well, 'tis a good time to start."

She didn't question him why, but she knew from watching the men at both her da's keep and Dornoch that too much fine Scottish whisky could make one do and say things they wouldna otherwise.

She must remember that. She'd been able to keep her thoughts away from the draw of the man sitting across from her by concentrating on the game.

Duncan returned to the table and handed her a cup, about half full of the brown liquid. She sniffed, and her eyes watered as she made a face. "I doona ken. 'Tis verra strong."

He took his seat and smiled at her. "Take a sip."

Holding her nose like a bairn would be too awkward, so she brought the cup to her lips and took a sip. The liquid burned her mouth and left a trail of heat all the way to her stomach. She inhaled deeply and waved her hand in front of her mouth. "'Twas quite hot."

His grin made her smile. "Aye, if ye've ne'er had whisky before, 'tis quite an experience." He took a sip of his drink and put the cup down on the table. "Do ye wish to continue playing?"

"Aye. Right now, we're even. Shall we say whoever wins the next round is the better player?" She took another sip. This one wasn't so hard to get down. "I think I'm getting used to this," she said holding up her cup.

"Just be careful, lass. 'Twill hit ye all at once. We doona want ye singing at the top of yer voice to wake the entire keep."

She laughed. "Nay. Ye doona want to hear me sing even if I wasna sipping whisky."

They started another game, Elsbeth taking a sip or two while they played. The warmth from the whisky was relaxing her, making her feel less uneasy with the two of them being alone together.

"Ye mentioned yer sister a few times. Ye are twins?" Duncan asked as he moved a pawn.

"Aye. Her name is Ainslee, and she is married to Laird Sutherland. But I think I told ye that before."

"Do ye look alike, then?"

Elsbeth laughed and took a swallow. "Ye think I looked like the lass ye were trying to steal? Well, I have no idea how that lass looks, but my sister and I look exactly alike." She took another sip. "'Tis getting warm in here."

Before Duncan could respond, she added, "In fact, we look so much alike that we switched places at her wedding."

Duncan's brows rose to his hairline. "Ye did?"

"Aye," she giggled. Suddenly the entire thing seemed

funny. Certainly not as she had felt that day. "Laird Sutherland was to marry me, but the mon scared me to death. So, on the day of the wedding, Ainslee and I switched places." She took a sip of whisky and smirked at their perfidy.

His slight grin grew to a full smile. "So, he married yer sister?"

"Aye." Another sip.

"What did the laird have to say about that?"

Elsbeth shrugged. "He acted as though he was mad, but he had already discovered our ruse before the vows were spoken."

"Ah, so it sounds as though he had reason to believe she was the better match for him."

Elsbeth shrugged and looked down at the chess board, but 'twas a bit wavy. Mayhap, she was just too tired to continue the game. She picked up her cup and was surprised to see 'twas empty.

She began to giggle again and looked over at Duncan who viewed her with a sparkle in his eyes. "Are ye feeling all right, lass?"

She nodded and hiccupped. "Fine." At least that was what she thought she said. "I'd feel better if ye would sit still, though."

Duncan stood. "All right, lass, I believe the whisky has hit ye hard. We can finish the game tomorrow, but I think for tonight I better escort ye to yer bedchamber."

He pulled her chair out, and she stood. And swayed.

He caught her around the waist. "Steady now, lass. Go slow."

They made their way through the now empty keep. She had a bit of trouble maneuvering the steps until Duncan reached down, scooped her in his arms, and carried her upstairs.

"Ye shoduna' fo thish," she said.

He laughed again. "I can hardly understand what ye said. But 'tis a much quicker way to get ye to yer bedchamber."

She shook her head then held her stomach. The dizziness made her feel a tad nauseous. "Ye canna come into my bedchamber, ye ken."

"Aye, lass. I ken."

Once they arrived at the door to her bedchamber, he set her down and opened the door. "Are ye all right to get yerself to bed?"

She looked up at that handsome face. Using the tip of her finger, she traced the scar that he'd hidden beneath his short beard. "How did ye get this?"

"I dinna duck quick enough on the battlefield." Instead of being terse with her, he continued to smile at her question.

She grinned and leaned into him. "I think it makes ye look verra dangerous. And handsome."

Duncan played with the hairs that had fallen from her plait onto her shoulders. "Dangerous, eh?"

After a quick nod, she reached for his shoulders to keep the corridor from spinning. An idea popped into her head that she probably should have ignored, but for some reason it seemed a perfectly good idea.

"Do ye want to kiss me?"

Duncan's body stiffened, and he wrapped his arms around her body. "Why would ye ask that?"

Elsbeth shrugged. Mayhap it wasn't such a good idea. Mayhap it was. "I think 'tis a good idea."

Running his finger up and down her cheek felt so good,

she leaned into him again until she was resting completely against his warm, hard, strong body. She moved her hands from his shoulders and linked her fingers behind his neck. "Do ye think 'tis a good idea?"

"Aye and nay." He dragged the words out.

"What does that mean?"

"I think kissing ye is a grand idea, one of the best in fact, but doing it when ye are not in yer normal state of mind is not a good thing. I'm not in the habit of taking advantage of lasses who have had too much to drink."

She pushed him back, and then grabbed his shoulders again when things started to spin again. "I haven't had too much to drink."

"Aye, ye have. Since ye ne'er had whisky before, I shouldn't have put so much into yer cup. That and it being late appears the spirits have hit ye hard."

The hair at the back of his head always interested her. She twirled the locks with her fingers. Soft, so very soft. "So that means ye doona want to kiss me?"

He brushed the loose hairs from her forehead. "Verra much so, my lady. I ne'er think of much of anything when yer near than kissing ye. But I doona want to take advantage of ye. Being a gentleman, I insist ye go into yer room and lock the door." With those words, he turned her body and placing his hands on her shoulders, gave her a slight nudge.

She took one stumbling step, so he once more scooped her into his arms and carried her to the bed. Placing her there, he leaned down and kissed her on the forehead. "There's yer kiss, lass." He pulled up the bedcovers and stepped back. "Now go to sleep."

* * *

CURSING himself for being ten times a fool, Duncan shut the door to Elsbeth's room and practically raced for his own bedchamber before he changed his mind about his honor. He never should have let her drink the whisky. She would pay the price in the morning, he was certain, but it also turned her into a siren whose song would crash him into pieces as much as the legend foretold.

Once he climbed into bed, all he could think of was how much he wanted Elsbeth's warm, soft body lying right next to him. He tossed one way, then the other. Nothing helped.

He flipped onto his back and tucked his hands behind his head, staring at the canopy. In another day or two, they would be able to leave for Perth. There was no doubt in his mind that he wanted her for his wife.

With the roads somewhat dry, it would take about four days to get to Perth. And three nights.

That would give him time with Elsbeth to convince her of the wisdom of not entering a convent but marrying him. mayhap Alastair was correct and 'twas a romance gone wrong that drove the lass to the life she was headed to.

He rolled onto his stomach, resting his chin on his fists. Tomorrow he would tell the lass she should prepare to leave for Perth the day after. He would take a few men with him for protection, but from what he knew of the area they would be traveling in, things were currently quiet.

Four days and three nights to woo the lass and bring her right back to Freuchie Castle as his wife.

Wife.

Aye, the word itself sounded good. The woman attached to the word was even better. Beautiful, loving, charming, caring. There were many more words that made up Lady Elsbeth Johnstone. If all the men at

Dornoch were so blind as to let Elsbeth head off to a convent, then he would take advantage of their neglect. And stupidity.

He finally fell asleep, only to awaken with a stiff cock and memories of dreams about Elsbeth right alongside him in bed. The dreams had been so real, he glanced over expecting to see her there.

Nay. He tossed the bedcovers aside and quickly washed and dressed for the day. He would tell Elsbeth when she came down to break her fast that they would leave for Perth the following day.

He'd have to see which men would be best suited to travel with them. He also had to arrange with the cook to take food with them so they didn't have to hunt for their every meal.

Feeling sure of his plan to convince Elsbeth that she belonged here at Freuchie Castle with him, he left his room and hurried down the stairs.

The woman who'd been on his mind all night sat at a table near the dais. Her bent elbows rested on the table, her hands propping up her head. He took a seat alongside her on the bench. "Good morn, lass."

She groaned. "Please doona talk to me."

He couldn't help but laugh, remembering many times in his youth when he had mornings like the one she was currently suffering from. "I have good news for ye."

Slowly, she turned her head toward him. Her eyes were bloodshot and her face as pale as snow. "What is the good news?"

"Are ye sure yer up to it?"

She growled.

"Sorry, lass. I just wanted to tell ye that ye need to

recover from yer illness quickly since I've determined that we can leave for Perth tomorrow."

She started to smile, then her eyes grew wide, and she hopped up from the bench and stumbled away, racing out of the great hall, the palm of her hand clamped over her mouth.

He hoped she'd made it to the garderobe in time.

7

'Twas hopefully a good sign that the morning the group from Freuchie Castle prepared to leave for Perth the air was warmer than usual, and the sun shone down on them.

Since Elsbeth's horse had been left behind with her escort on the night she was dragged from her tent, Duncan gave her a tour of the stables at Freuchie Castle to find a horse she was comfortable with.

She'd always been a strong rider, so she had no trouble choosing an animal.

"I can have the groom tack this one for ye if that's what ye want," Duncan said over her shoulder as she stroked her palm down the sleek black palfrey's velvety nose.

"Aye. He's a beauty. What's his name?"

"Grisone."

She leaned in close so the animal could smell her breath. "'Tis a pleasure to meet ye, Grisone. Are ye going to give me a nice ride to Perth?"

The beautiful gelding shook his head, then nudged her

shoulder with his nose. "Aye. It looks to me like yer wanting a treat, eh?" She pulled an apple from her dress pocket and held it out for the horse.

"We will get along just fine," she said to Duncan as the horse munched on the piece of fruit.

Once the galloway was loaded down with the food and other things the group would need for the trip, Duncan called for them all to mount so they could be on their way.

Elsbeth would not ride on a side saddle which she considered much too dangerous, so she'd managed to pilfer a pair of trews from one of the smaller men in the keep. Earlier, she'd pulled them on under her dress. If Duncan was surprised at that, he didn't show it. Instead, he nodded at her when she swung her leg over the horse, most likely giving everyone in the area a peek at her garb.

"Good idea, lass."

She nodded her thanks and wrapped an arisadh around her and looked up at the castle where she'd spent over a week. It amazed her that she was almost as sad leaving Freuchie as she'd been leaving Dornoch. Of course, 'twas not necessary to say goodbye to her sister again, though.

Despite being a captive—no matter what Duncan said— her time here had been pleasant. Except, of course, the sour stomach and pounding headache she'd suffered the morning after her introduction to Scottish whisky. Never again, she'd promised herself.

God's bones. Were those tears threatening to gather in her eyes? 'Twas foolish. Blinking rapidly lest Duncan see her and put too much importance on her leave-taking, she offered him a smile. "Are we ready, Laird?"

He studied her for a few moments, his face a picture of concern. "Are ye sure, lass? This is truly what ye want?"

Curse the man. Why would he say that? 'Twas obvious he'd seen her tears. Well, she had made up her mind already and suffered through saying goodbye to her beloved sister and her sweet nieces and nephews. This would be no worse. She nodded and moved her horse away from the stable door. "Aye. I'm ready."

They had a total of five men with them, the packhorse and Elsbeth. She rode between Daniel and Gregory, with Duncan at the front and the last two men who'd been with the laird the night she'd been taken, behind her. She was certainly well protected.

They traveled over soggy ground but met with no flooded areas. The air was warm, the breeze on her face welcoming. The group made good time, only stopping briefly for her to relieve herself. 'Twas embarrassing knowing the men had to be told each time she needed to stop. She tried to make it easier on herself by refusing the waterskin when offered to her. But then her mouth was so dry she wasn't sure 'twas worth denying it.

Thoughts of this decision torturing her as she rode all morning, she was relieved when Duncan raised his hand as a signal to stop. Having not slept well the night before with everything on her mind, she was a bit weary, and glad for the break. As it was close to noon, she assumed they were stopping to eat. Her assumption was correct when Duncan hopped from his horse and after hobbling the animal, headed to the galloway.

She climbed from Grisone, her legs giving out for a moment as her feet hit the ground. She clung to her horse until she felt stronger, not wanting to appear weak in front of the men. 'Twas bad enough that they probably already thought she possessed a bladder the size of a pea.

"Are ye well, Elsbeth?" Duncan asked as he joined her alongside Grisone, as she pretended to soothe the horse while she was actually allowing her legs to return to normal so she didn't fall flat on her face when she moved.

"Aye. Just fine, Laird."

He held out his hand. "Come join us for a meal. I have bread, cheese, and apples Beatrice packed for us."

She nodded and took one step and stopped. "I will join ye in a minute."

Apparently, her ruse didn't work because Duncan smiled then extended his elbow. "Allow me to escort ye, my lady."

Her eyes narrowed, but 'twould not be wise to act so foolishly and stumble when she didn't want to appear frail. She took his arm and leaned a bit heavier than normal as they walked, pleasantly conversing about the morning's ride.

* * *

DUNCAN KEPT his smile inside as they moved to a cleared space where several downed trees made it a nice, safe place for them to eat. 'Twas proud he was of the lass not wanting to show any weakness.

The area of the woods where they'd stopped was off the more traveled road, and quite dense which provided good cover.

Although he'd ridden at the front of the group for most of the morning, he did on occasion switch places with Gregory so he could ride next to Elsbeth. He hadn't traveled much with women, but he remembered from their trek with her to Freuchie over a week ago that she would need to stop more than the men. He assumed she would be more comfortable telling him she needed a break than one of the other men.

Had they been without a lass, they wouldna even stop, but just veer off from the group and piss as they rode along. Things were much simpler for men, he had to admit.

They all settled, with most of the group sitting on the ground. Duncan took the food out of the bag and passed it around. The men didn't speak much, but Elsbeth seemed to be full of questions.

"Do ye ken when we will arrive in Perth?"

He just stared at her, her beautiful eyes almost taking his breath away. The depth of the woods with the sun peeking through the leaves turned her eyes into a moss green. A more beautiful lass he'd never seen. He blew out a deep breath at his foolishness and returned his attention to the bag. He pulled out the bread, cheese, and apples, handing some to her.

"The entire trip should take no more than four days. Maybe less if we continue to be blessed with this weather and a lack of rain." He took a sip of ale from the wineskin. "But doona count on it. Downpours such as we saw the last week can happen anytime ye ken, since ye've lived in the Highlands yer whole life."

She pondered that for a few moments, then asked, "Are the areas we are traveling through considered safe?"

Duncan chewed and swallowed the piece of apple he'd just bit into. "As safe as any other area in the Highlands. With it being summer, reivers are busy and that can always be a dangerous situation to run into." He patted her knee, wanting to leave his hand there, but reluctantly removed it. "Doona fash yerself, Elsbeth. Even though we are only five men, we are all well trained. It doesn't pay to ever let yer guard down."

Elsbeth nodded and tore off a piece of bread as she looked off into the woods. Was she anxious about the travel time because she was eager to reach the convent and begin her new life? Or was she considering that mayhap she should turn around and return to Freuchie with him?

Doona be a fool.

'Twas all wishful thinking on his part. If he talked to her more about what she expected from the convent and what she left behind at Dornoch, he might uncover why she was determined to see this plan through.

"How long did ye live with yer sister in Dornoch?"

Elsbeth swallowed a bite of cheese. Although he wanted to hear the answers to his question, he was struck by the tip of her pink tongue scooping up a wee piece of cheese from her lips. Lips he wanted to taste again.

"She and Haydon married a tad bit more than three years past. My da permitted me to stay with her after the wedding until she felt settled."

"And it took her three years to feel settled?" he asked with a grin. "From what ye told me about her switching places with ye at her wedding, I assumed she was more resilient."

A sly smile graced her lips. "Nay, she dinna need me for three years, to be sure. Ainslee was always the leader of the two of us. mayhap in the beginning she felt the need to keep me close, since as twins we had been together since before we were born." She tossed the core from her apple over her shoulder. "'Tis a unique connection."

"Aye, I'm sure of that. I canna imagine looking at my

own face every day with there being no looking glass around."

Elsbeth laughed. "I ne'er thought of that, but 'tis true." She looked up again at the sun, a smile on her lips. Her beauty grew even more radiant as she allowed the warmth to bathe her face.

He tried to make the next question appear casual but wasn't sure it came across that way. "So, what about yer da? Wasna he planning on another alliance by marrying ye off?"

She shrugged. "I stayed with Ainslee for several months before I traveled back to visit my da." She sighed. "He insisted I return. I stayed for as long as I could, but I had promised Ainslee I would return in time for her bairn to be born. Since 'twas wintertime, I dinna make it to Dornoch in time for the birth, but I was able to spend a lot of time with my niece, Lady Susana Sutherland."

"And I take it yer da had no success in finding ye a husband while ye stayed with him?" If the lass noticed he'd been plying her with the same question, she didn't mention it.

She smiled again. "He tried. But no one caught my heart."

"Yer heart?" He was afraid he shouted that since two of the men looked over at them. "What has that to do with marriage?"

Elsbeth reared back. "I have no intention of marrying for any other reason than love."

He shook his head. "Nay, lass. A woman's duty is to marry to make a strong alliance with her family and produce bairns to inherit her husband's lairdship. Ye want a mon who can provide for ye and protect ye and give ye strong bairns." He chuckled. "Ye are still tied up with yer childhood stories of romance and such other nonsense."

One look at her face and he knew he'd just made a very, very big mistake. She raised her chin and stared at him. "My sister and her husband are besotted with each other. The laird's brother and his wife are the same. Unlike yer idea of duty, I feel if I canna have love in my marriage, I see no reason for it." With those words, she stood, brushed off her dress, and looked down at him. "I need some private time for a minute, Laird."

Stunned at her words, he watched her lovely hips sway as she marched off as if going into battle. Love? He'd always planned when he married, he would hold affection for his wife. Respect, surely. Caring as well. But love? Nay that's what killed his father.

He gathered the remains of their meal and returned the uneaten food to the bag strapped to the galloway.

"What were ye and the lass arguing about?" Gregory asked as he walked up to Duncan checking the straps on Elsbeth's horse.

"We were no' arguing." He gave the strap a good tug.

"It sounded like it to me." Gregory nodded in the direction Elsbeth had just stormed off to. "Looks like it too."

"Well, then ye need to clean out yer ears since yer hearing things that aren't there." He walked off in the opposite direction of Elsbeth to relieve himself.

Once finished, he called them all to get ready to leave. Within minutes, Elsbeth had returned and strode to her horse without giving him a glance.

Fine. If that was how the lass wanted it, then that was fine. Very fine. Very, very fine, indeed.

The afternoon hours passed slowly. He stayed at the

front of the group and was more than a wee bit annoyed at the sound of Elsbeth's laughter as she spoke with Daniel, then John, and finally Kevin.

His mood grew grumpier as the ride continued. Christ's toes, it sounded like they were in the middle of a party back there. Were the men watching out for danger, or just riding along like a bunch of lasses as if they were in a park in the middle of Edinburgh?

'Twas time to remind them that this was not a lively jaunt, but a serious trip through areas that might not be so friendly. He held his arm up for them to stop.

"Why ye stopping?" John called from behind him.

"We need a break." He steered his horse into the woods and jumped down. The others, looking confused, followed suit. He growled when Daniel moved over to Elsbeth's horse and helped her down.

He faced his men and the lass, his hands on his hips. "I want to remind ye all that we have no assurance that the land we travel, which is probably part of the small patch of the Gordon clan, is friendly. Ye are making enough noise back there that they probably heard ye in Perth." He waved his arms around like a madman. The men and Elsbeth all stared at him. Kevin had the nerve to smile. Good. He was in a mood to punch someone's face.

Before he gave into that impulse, he turned and stormed off deeper into the woods. Since they'd stopped, he might as well get rid of his own piss.

Instead of returning immediately, he took a walk along a creek that ran through the area. Maybe being away from the lass would calm him down. Thoughts of her certainly had twisted him into knots. He turned quickly, his hand on his sword when he heard footsteps behind him.

"Are ye well, Duncan?" Elsbeth's soft voice rolled over him like a silky spring rain.

Aside from feeling like a fool?

"Aye. I'm sorry for that rant back there."

She moved closer to him. "Do ye think we might be in danger here?" The worry in her beautiful green eyes tore him up. The last thing he wanted to do was frighten the lass. But he did need to impress upon her that any travel from a man's own lands was always fraught with potential danger.

Unable to help himself, he reached out and tucked a loose strand of curly red hair behind her ear. "'Tis always good to be aware of where ye are. Ye've traveled before, ye must ken these things."

Standing next to her, able to breathe in her faint scent of flowers even though he stood outside, was wreaking havoc with his blood supply. God, he wanted her. There was no reason to deny it.

But the lass wanted love. 'Twas not something he would be able to give her. Even if he were able to talk her out of the convent.

"Aye," she said. "I ken we got a bit loud back there, but Daniel is quite funny in his observations. It did make the time pass quicker, I must say."

Her cheeks grew red as she continued. "I hope yer mood doesn't come from our conversation before. I dinna mean to be so forceful with ye. I ken it makes no difference to ye if ye have love in yer marriage or no'. And since I'm headed to a life of service, I have no need to worry about that myself. There really was no purpose to the disagreement."

Ach. Even hearing her say those words shamed him. She didn't belong in a convent. But from what she expected from a husband, she would never belong with him, either.

"Let's head back to the others. We need to put a few more hours in while the weather is good." He took her arm to keep her from stumbling on rocks and roots. Even though he told himself she had found him without a problem.

The rest of the men looked at him warily when they returned, but no one said a word about his outburst. Good. 'Twas important to remind them ev'er once in a while that he was their laird and they'd sworn their allegiance to him which included listening to his commands.

"Let us depart. I hope to make a few more miles before dark."

Not giving the men time to move, Duncan walked over to Elsbeth. Putting his hands on her waist, he lifted her into her saddle. Obviously startled, she had to grab the horse's head to keep from sliding off the animal. He turned and stared at the rest of the men daring with his eyes and tight lips for any of them to comment.

Confident that they'd been assured of his role as laird and leader, he strode to his horse, mounted, then signaled for them to move forward.

8

'Twas the last full day of travel. At least that was what Duncan told Elsbeth when they set off that morning. The night had been spent on damp ground, with a light sprinkle of rain almost all night. Duncan had erected her tent again, but the chill never seemed to leave her body.

She was weary of travel and wanted nothing more than to sleep in a real bed. She must have said it out loud because Duncan placed his hands on her waist to hoist her up onto the horse and said, "Tonight we shall stop at a public house I ken for a hot meal and a bed."

She turned, excitement building in her. "For real? And mayhap a hot bath, also?"

He offered that smile that always twisted her insides. "Aye, lass. I must admit ye have been verra patient on this trip. I ken of few lasses who would not be howling their distress with sleeping in the woods and eating the same thing for days. Ye would make a good warrior."

Flattered by the compliment, she smiled. "Thank ye,

Laird, but I fear were the position offered to me, I would be forced to decline."

His smile drooped. "Because ye are determined to enter the convent?"

Her laughter burst forth. "That, too, Laird, but also the fact that I would ne'er be able to lift one of yer swords, let alone swing it with enough power and skill to keep from having my head separated from my body."

"Aye, there is that." He lifted her and placed her on the horse. She immediately felt the loss of warmth and connection to Duncan as she settled onto the saddle and wrapped the arisadh around her, the large garment covering her body and head. The natural oils in the plaid would offer some protection from the light rain that had continued.

Things had changed among the group over the last few days. The men didn't tease her or offer to help her on or off her horse. She considered it the result of Duncan's lecture about paying more attention to their surroundings, but deep inside she feared the men were leaving her be because Duncan claimed her as his own.

That would never do, of course, since she was only a day away from her destination. Her stomach clenched at the thought, and she considered for a minute that her breakfast might make a reappearance and land on the poor horse's neck.

She finally admitted this morning that the closer they got to Perth, the more she had begun to question her decision. But returning to Dornoch with nothing there for her, or to Lochwood Tower where her da would certainly marry her off with or without her permission posthaste, were not options she could accept. It seemed her only choice was now the convent.

She would enjoy a life of peace, silence, and helping others.

'Tis a long life, Elsbeth. Will ye allow yer stubbornness to make ye unhappy for the rest of yer life?

Ach, she wished the voice inside her head would cease to annoy her.

The few hours since dawn passed in a relatively pleasant manner. The ride first thing in the morn was easier on her body than the end of the day when she was sore, tired, and bored. Miles and miles of woods and hills made for a very uninteresting journey.

About the time she had considered asking Duncan to stop since she was wiggling on the saddle, trying to ignore her body's need, he raised his hand for the group to halt. He turned his horse and addressed them. "We're close to the small village outside of Perth. I ken there is a public house with an inn, and a few crofters who sell their wares, hoping to wrestle coin from travelers before they hit Perth where so much more is available.

"The plan is to stop in the village for the rest of the day to allow us to enjoy a hot meal and a restful night out of the cold. 'Twill also give our brave lass a chance to prepare herself for arrival at the convent."

He appeared to spit out the last few words. While grateful to be able to bathe and put on clean clothes—minus the trews—before meeting Sister Albert, the truth of the matter was she felt terrified.

Once the group left her in Perth and returned to Freuchie Castle, there was no changing her mind. From what Sister Albert had written to her, within weeks of arriving, the bishop would attend them to have Elsbeth take her final vows.

Final vows.

It sounded so … final. Well, she reassured herself, if her da had forced her to marry, that would have been final, also. With a sniff—not tears she assured herself—she lifted her chin and continued following Duncan to the village.

Her spirits picked up as they rode over a hill and the tiny village sat before them. Nestled in the hills, it was lovely, almost as she'd imagined in the fairy tales her governess had told her and Ainslee about in the evenings before the fire in the girls' bedchamber.

At least a dozen thatched-roof houses were scattered about. Small children ran around chasing each other and a few cats. Women draped laundered clothing over bushes. The light rain had finally stopped, and the bit of sun peeking from behind the clouds would help dry the clothing.

All the dwellings had large fenced in areas behind their cottages that housed livestock. Sheep seemed to be the prevailing animal, which led her to believe that these crofters would have much to offer in the way of woolen garments.

Not that she would need any new clothes, herself. Sister Albert explained that she would be provided with a coarse hair dress for daily use. Her spirts drooped, and she felt itchy already.

Duncan led them to a stable where they all gratefully dismounted, with Duncan, of course, helping her down. Used to how little her legs worked after riding, he chatted with her for a few minutes while she regained some strength.

"Now that the rain has stopped, I would like to visit the crofters for a short time."

"Aye. I will go with ye." He stuck his elbow out and she settled herself next to him as they strolled away from the stable toward several crofters set up in the center of the village.

* * *

This could very well be the last time he was able to offer his arm to the lass. After visiting with the crofters, they would enjoy a meal better than what they'd been eating, and soon thereafter, sleep in a real bed.

By his calculations, they would arrive before noon in Perth. A gloom had settled over him the last few hours. If he talked Elsbeth into giving up this plan of hers, could he offer marriage, knowing he would not allow himself to love her?

Nay. She would ask, and he couldna lie to her. But if she questioned him about love, it would mean that she had feelings for him and wanted them returned. He stole a glance at her as her eyes darted back and forth, looking at all the offerings. His stomach twisted and his heart pounded.

Was he already in trouble with his feelings for the lass?

"Oh, look, Duncan." She pointed at a table that had an array of small carved animals. She dragged him over to the man behind the table.

"Maura's da makes these little toys. He sells quite a bit of them in Dornoch," she said as she admired the man's work.

"Ah, I take it Maura is one of yer friends at the castle?"

She shrugged and picked up a small horse. "A friend, and also married to the brother of my sister's husband." She turned to him, frowning. "Did I say that right? Maura is married to Conall who is Haydon's brother. Haydon is

Ainslee's husband." She laughed and shook her head. "No matter. Maura is still a friend whatever her relationship to me is."

Elsbeth was adorable. Like an eager bairn, she picked up various animals to admire, exclaiming over each piece until Duncan thought the crofter's chest would explode with pride.

"Would ye like me to buy one for ye, Elsbeth?" He carried enough coin on him to pay for food and lodging at the public house, and still have enough to make her happy if she wanted one of them.

Her eyes lit up, then dimmed. "Nay. I wouldna have use for it. I must give up all my possessions when we arrive at the convent."

He suddenly had the urge to grab her hand, drag her to the stable, toss her onto her horse and race back to Freuchie Castle. He'd made her prisoner once; he could do it again.

He took a deep breath. "Let us head to the public house. I'm sure ye are feeling hunger by now. 'Tis been a while since we broke our fast."

She put the animal down and smiled at the man. "These are truly lovely. Thank ye for letting me admire them."

She linked her arm through his again and they passed the rest of the crofters by. He noted she no longer glanced at the tables; her eyes remained on the public house in the short distance beyond.

Even though the place was in a very small village outside of a large town, they found the building to be clean and the food enjoyable. They both ordered pottage, which when arrived looked and smelled wonderful. It was accompanied by dark bread and freshly churned butter, and a heaping dish of pickled vegetables.

"Ye ken we ne'er finished our last game of chess. Right now, it stands one to one," Duncan said once they'd taken the last bite of their meal.

"Aye. They may have a chess board here, but I would prefer a walk around the village if ye doona mind. I'm a bit weary, but I think if I sit here too comfortably, trying to focus on chess, I will fall asleep. 'Twill be so nice to sleep in a bed."

The word *bed* had his blood flowing southward. If he were to spend the rest of the day with Elsbeth and then watch her close the door to the room he would secure for her, he needed to get his body under control. "Aye, I think a stroll around the village is a good thing."

He tossed coins onto the table, and they left the public house after Duncan arranged for her to have a room. He decided to soothe his sanity by sleeping in the public house stable with the rest of his men.

This time, instead of visiting with the crofters, they circled the entire village. Truth be told he was having a hard time making conversation since all he wanted to do was take the lass by the shoulders and shake some sense into her.

How could his feelings for a lass he'd only known for a couple of weeks be so strong? He'd met plenty of lasses and had bedded enough of them too. But none had e'er caught his eye or raised the feelings of protection and caring that he battled every day since he'd met Elsbeth.

They both apparently didn't want to discuss the next day, since Elsbeth commented on the animals they passed, the snug little cottages, the hills surrounding them, the warm air, and how much she looked forward to her bath and a soft bed.

God's toes he wished she'd stop saying that word.

He found he was unable to utter more than an 'aye' or a 'nay' as she rambled on. He finally realized her rambling was just that. She appeared nervous and kept taking deep breaths.

He groaned with relief when she suggested they return to the public house so she could enjoy her bath before they ate supper and retired for the night.

At least she didn't mention 'bed' again.

* * *

Elsbeth had never made such a fool of herself as she had during the stroll with Duncan. The very large word 'convent' stood between them like a brick wall, and no matter how much she tried to put thoughts of tomorrow off, they always arrived back in her head to encourage another bout of inane chatter.

With relief, she parted from him to find her room where the innkeeper's wife assured her the bath she'd been looking forward to was ready. She waved Duncan off and ascended the stairs.

She stayed in the bath until the water was quite cold and her fingers all shriveled. After drying off, she rummaged through the bag Duncan had removed from the galloway with her personal items in it. She brushed her hair, plaited the wet strands, and flipped it to her back. 'Twas nice to put on a clean dress, the other one dirty from days on the trip.

Duncan sat at the same table where they'd eaten their lunch. The four men who had been with them since Freuchie Castle occupied the other chairs surrounding the table. They all held cups of ale in their hands, and based on their jocularity, they might have been at it for some time.

"It looks like ye are all enjoying some rest time," she said as she sat in the chair Duncan held out for her.

"Aye, lass," Kevin said. "We hope to get a game of darts or ringing the bull going with some of the villagers after supper."

"I remember my da playing those games when he would take us to the village pub. Ainslee and I watched, but I always brought my chess board to entice someone to play."

"Ye are a chess player, then?" Daniel asked.

"Aye." Duncan said, smiling at her. "The lady is a fine chess player. She beat me once, and I beat her once."

Gregory raised his ale cup. "Well done, lass. Not many in the keep can beat our laird."

Elsbeth dipped her head. "Thank ye. Do any of ye play?"

The men all looked at each other and shook their heads. "Nay," John said. "Our laird keeps us much too busy training to have time for games."

Duncan huffed. "Ach. Ye liar. Ye doona want to play such games because it requires ye to think."

"There is that too," Kevin said with a loud guffaw and a slap on John's back.

They ordered their food and had a repeat of what had been served at the nooning. That was fine with Elsbeth because it was warm and tasty, and she didn't have to sit on the ground to eat it.

She and Duncan watched the men from their group and some of the village men line up for the dart game. After some encouragement, Duncan joined them while Elsbeth admired the man from behind. His broad shoulders blocked out the dart board as he flicked the dart with his strong arm.

His muscled legs and bottom outlined so well in his tartan trews held her attention much more than it should have.

The game grew more raucous as the men challenged each other, and numerous drinks to the men's health were offered as each new round of ale appeared.

Duncan left the game at one point and sat at the table with her. "I think it might be a good idea for ye to retire, lass. Things are getting more than lively, and I dinna like ye being here with all these men in their cups."

"I think ye have a good point." She stood and shook out her skirts.

"I'll escort ye to yer room." He took her arm, and they climbed the stairs to the bedchamber floor. "Which is yers?"

She led him to the room she'd been assigned and placed her hand on the latch, which was suddenly covered by Duncan's large hand. "Be sure to lock yer door securely."

Elsbeth nodded, suddenly feeling as if she would burst into tears. 'Twas her last night with Duncan. She had no idea what possessed her, but she leaned up on her toes, grasped the back of his neck with her hand and placed her lips on his.

If he'd been surprised, it passed quickly because he wrapped his arm around her waist and pulled her flush against him. His warm lips covered hers with hunger. He nipped at her lip, and she opened to enjoy the invasion of his tongue. He tasted of all the ale he'd drunk.

He released her mouth and cupped her face in his large hands. "Ah, lass, I want ye so much, but the only way I can take ye is if ye give up this convent idea and marry me."

She had to admit she was wavering. She pulled back and whispered. "Do ye love me?"

9

ater he would swear his heart came to an abrupt halt when she asked *do ye love me?* Was she changing her mind? Or was she testing him?

After a few moments, she'd said, "Nay, Duncan, if ye did, ye wouldn't hesitate." She'd shaken her head and opened the door. "I wish ye good night."

He'd been left staring at the old, scarred wooden door. He'd run his fingers through his hair and took a gulp of air that he'd seemed to be missing since she'd asked the question.

With a heavy heart, he'd walked away from her room. Instead of returning to the hilarity that was downstairs, he'd walked out of the building, around the corner to the stable and sat against a wall, his head back, legs bent, his wrists resting on his knees.

Do ye love me?

. . .

THE NEXT MORNING arrived much too soon, and not soon enough. He didn't sleep more than a few minutes, tossing on the pile of hay he'd used for a bed.

The men snored away, sleeping off all the drink they'd had. He stood and brushed himself off, pieces of hay floating in the air. The sun was just creeping over the horizon. He gathered his things and took a walk to the creek about half a mile behind the stable.

The cold water felt good on his face, waking him up and helping to shake off some of the doldrums he'd awoken with. He stood with his hands on his hips and looked out over the small village.

Times were when he wished he was merely a farmer, with a pleasant, uncomplicated wife, a farm to tend to, and bairns to raise. No responsibilities for other people. No concern for clan clashes or a king to keep happy. No woman who was driving him mad.

Shaking off his peculiar mood, he traipsed back to the stable to see Elsbeth standing at the entrance.

"Ah, yer up already, lass."

She nodded. "I dinna sleep verra well."

Ye are no' the only one.

"I assume we will be leaving soon?" Her words were not quite as strong as Duncan would have liked. He was quite sure she was still doubtful about this whole thing. He could keep her here if he only told her he loved her and wanted to marry her.

But he couldn't lie. If they did marry, the time might come when he did think of her in a more romantic way, but she would know from the start that she wasn't getting the love she claimed her sister and sister-by-marriage were getting from their besotted husbands.

She would be crushed, and he couldna do that to her.

He sighed. "Aye. I just need to get these dunderheads up." He kicked at Kevin's foot.

The man opened his eyes. "Time already?"

"Aye. Get yer mates up. If ye want to break yer fast before we leave, ye need to get up now."

Duncan joined Elsbeth who had moved outside the stable. "Are ye ready to break yer fast?"

"Aye." She walked beside him, the silence between them overwhelming.

All the lass consumed was part of an oatcake and a few sips of ale. They didn't talk as they ate. The other men arrived and ate a quick bowl of porridge and a few cups of ale.

"'Tis time to leave." Duncan stood and headed to the door. He could hear Elsbeth's footsteps behind him, soon followed by grunts and groans from his men who most likely were suffering the aftereffects of the liveliness the night before.

'Twas a quiet group that rode the few miles to Perth. No laughter, jokes, or comments. The men were suffering, and Duncan was thinking. Elsbeth looked more distressed the farther they rode.

Close to noon, they arrived on the outskirts of Perth. They stopped at a public house since they were all ready for the nooning. Duncan helped Elsbeth off her horse, and they joined the others at a table.

"Do ye have a direction for this convent?" Duncan asked.

"Aye. I have my last letter from Sister Albert. She said 'tis on the corner of East Street and High Street." She shrugged. "That's all the information I have."

"Doona fash yerself, lass, we'll ask the innkeeper before

we leave. Even though Perth is a good size, we shouldna have a problem finding it. Is there a name for it?"

"Aye. The Sisters of the Poor."

Fitting. She would be poor the rest of her life. Poor of everything a lass wanted. And deserved.

They all trooped out after receiving directions from the innkeeper. The entire group was glum. Even the bright sunshine didn't do anything to perk them up.

Following the map the man had drawn for them on the back of the missive Elsbeth had from Sister Albert, it took about twenty minutes to arrive at the building.

'Twas very old. Dark, and damp. They all stopped and stared. There was nothing identifying the place as a convent. In fact, it looked deserted. Elsbeth looked over at Duncan and attempted a smile. "Well, here we are."

No one moved. Or spoke. Finally, Elsbeth shifted to get off her horse. Duncan jumped from his and helped her down. Together, they climbed the steps to the front door. After a slight hesitation, Elsbeth dropped the knocker on the door, and they stepped back.

No answer.

Taking a deep breath, Elsbeth repeated the action. They waited a few minutes.

No answer.

She looked over at Duncan and frowned. This time he banged on the door with his fist, rather than using the knocker.

Nothing.

Elsbeth backed up and looked up at the outside of the building. Then she turned to Duncan. "Should I just enter?"

He had a very bad feeling about this. "Nay. Ye stay here, and I will go inside."

The old door rattled and squeaked as he pushed it open. The inside was dark, cold, and unwelcoming. He couldna leave Elsbeth here. He refused to leave her here. He walked a few steps on the stone floor waiting for someone to approach.

No one did.

Eventually, he toured the entire two-story house. Every room was empty of people, but full of furniture. He made his way downstairs and just as he reached the bottom stair, the front door opened and Elsbeth stuck her head in. "What are ye doing?"

"Looking the place over, but there isna anything to see."

* * *

Elsbeth rubbed her palms up and down her arms. The place was very uninviting. But even more notable was the fact that Duncan said after a tour of the building, he found no one there. How very odd.

She wasn't sure if it was disappointment or relief she felt. Most likely a bit of each. "I wonder where everyone is. If you say there is furniture, then mayhap they are all on an outing?"

Duncan looked around and shook his head. "Dinna ye say there were sick people here that needed tending to?"

"Aye."

"Then I doona think they are traipsing all o'er Perth on an outing."

She finally asked what she'd been afraid to ask. "What do I do now?"

If he and his men just rode off and left her, 'twould be even worse than she'd expected when she thought she would be welcomed. She fought down the tears that threatened. She'd worried about this decision, had to talk her sister and brother-by-marriage into it.

She'd been kidnapped, stranded at a strange keep for over a week, and then traveled to the convent to find it empty. 'Twas too much.

Elsbeth swallowed as she tried to keep the tears down, but it didn't work. She looked up at Duncan, and her chin quivered. He pulled her into his arms and held her while she cried. His warm hand settled on her head where he rubbed her scalp and murmured words she didn't hear.

She cried for the life and happiness her sister had that she never would. She cried for the strain of the last fortnight, and the long treks from Dornoch to Freuchie and then from there to Perth.

Now she had nothing, no one, and nowhere to go. The tears became genuine sobs. Duncan continued to offer solace, his chin resting on her head.

When her sobbing turned into hiccups, she drew back from Duncan and took the piece of linen he handed her. "What do I do now?"

He drew in a deep breath. "One thing for sure. Ye canna stay here."

Elsbeth closed her eyes in relief.

Duncan placed his hands on her shoulders, his brows almost reaching his hairline. "Surely you dinna think I would leave ye here?"

Using the now soggy linen, she wiped her nose and said, "I doona ken what to think." Her shoulders drooped. "I'm so verra weary."

"Aye, I understand. What I suggest we do is return to the public house and see if we can get some information on this place. Since ye received a letter from this sister with the directions, I'm assuming something unexpected happened."

Elsbeth nodded, all the strength leaving her. She hadn't realized how very distressed she'd been until she'd collapsed against Duncan. She was only too happy to have him take over and make the decisions about this mess.

They returned outside to the men all sitting on their horses and waiting. "Is everything well, lass? Ye look a tad upset," Gregory said.

Duncan lifted her and plopped her onto the horse. "We doona ken what the problem is. Right now, it appears no one is in the building. We need to determine if anyone in Perth is familiar with the place, and why it is empty."

By the time they returned to the public house, Elsbeth had a pounding headache. What she wanted more than anything—besides her sister—was to lie down in a dark room with a lavender-scented linen on her head. When she'd had these headaches before that always worked well.

"Ye aren't looking well, lass. Might I suggest we see if there is a room available for ye to lie down in for a while?"

Why did it always seem this man was able to read her mind? She smiled. "Aye. I was just thinking that. I find I have a rather bad headache."

Duncan placed his hand on her lower back and moved her forward toward the desk where the clerk stood. "I'd like a room for the lass if ye still have one open."

The man looked up and smiled at them. "Actually, I doona think the room ye left has even been cleaned yet, so ye are welcome to stay there for a while." He narrowed his eyes and looked closer at her. "Are ye well, lass? Ye look a bit upset."

"I just have a headache," she snapped, immediately sorry

for her response but anxious to get to the room and try to mayhap e'en take a nap and forget this entire morning.

God's bones. Forget the entire trip.

The man handed Duncan a key. They started toward the stairs when he turned back. "Is it possible to get a cool cloth with some lavender on it?"

Here he was, being nice again. Very nice. Just what she didn't need to add to her already confusing day.

"Aye. My wife surely has some. I'll send her up with it in a bit. She can help yer wife get settled."

Duncan nodded and walked Elsbeth up the stairs to the room. He used the key to open the door and moved aside to let her in. "Take as much time as ye need. In the meantime, I will see if I can gather any information on that convent."

Elsbeth reached out and touched his hand. "Thank ye so much, Duncan. I have ne'er felt so lost in my life."

"Ye will ne'er be lost while ye are with me." With those words he kissed her on the forehead and left. She looked at the bed and walked over to it, lying down gently to keep her head from moving too much.

'Twasn't more than about ten minutes when the innkeeper's wife arrived with the cloth. The cool linen felt good against her head. She thanked her and closed her eyes.

Before she knew it, she was fast asleep.

* * *

Duncan collapsed into the chair near the fireplace. The other men had settled at one of the tables. All looked to him. "What do we do now, Laird?" Kevin asked.

He ran his fingers through his hair. "One thing is certain; we canna leave the lass here."

"I doona think ye *ever* wanted to leave her here," Daniel said with a smirk.

Duncan glowered at him. "'Tis a serious situation. I must find out what happened at that house. The place was full of furniture and even food in the larder, but no one there." He shook his head. "Verra strange."

Just then, the innkeeper's wife came out of the kitchen, wiping her hands on her apron. "My husband tells me ye were asking about that building where the nuns live."

"Aye. We just came back from there and found it empty. Do ye ken anything about it?"

"Nay. But there's a mon who lives two houses down from there. His name is Darby. An old mon, been around for a long, long time. When he was out of coin from drinking too much, he would beg a meal from the nuns." She laughed. "He always told them he would pray for their souls. It seemed to me he needed more prayers for his soul than they did."

"Thank ye, mistress. I appreciate the information."

She placed her hands on her impressive hips. "Will ye be needing the room again tonight?"

It didn't look like the lass was going to be able to stay in the convent tonight. Or, hopefully, any night. He offered a quick prayer up for his soul. 'Twas possible there wasn't anything troublesome going on, but until they had some answers, Elsbeth needed a place to sleep. "Aye. Please keep the room, I will pay as soon as we ken how long we will need it."

The woman nodded and returned to her duties.

About two hours after Elsbeth had retired to the room, she slowly came down the stairs. She looked better, but still unsettled. Her eyes were no longer red and swollen.

Since Duncan hadn't wanted to question the old man Darby until Elsbeth could be with them, they all stayed in the public house, playing darts, drinking more ale, and passing time.

"Are ye feeling better, Elsbeth?" Duncan asked.

She nodded, but easily, as if she was still in some pain. "Did ye get any information?' she asked.

"Some. Come and sit down. mayhap a cup of tea would do ye well before we set out." The drink had been introduced to Scotland about twenty years before. It was still not widely available, but the innkeeper's wife had mentioned to him that she kept some tea leaves for her own use and if Elsbeth wanted to drink some she would make her a cup. 'Twas thought to be helpful for one's nerves.

"Aye. I would like that. We had tea once in a while at home in Lochwood Tower. Our cook liked the drink and kept it on hand."

Once Elsbeth was settled with her tea, Duncan related the information about the old man, Darby, and how he might have some information on where the nuns were.

"I doona think ye all need to come with us. I will escort Elsbeth back to the building and find this Darby," Duncan said to his men. "Doona spend the rest of the day drinking yer ale again. I have no idea what story we will be told, and what we will need to do."

"Aye," Daniel said.

Duncan escorted Elsbeth to the stable behind the public house, and they headed back to the building on East Street and High Street.

Elsbeth was quiet on the ride back, and he was concerned for her, knowing she must be feeling at a loss. She stared straight ahead as they rode through the town, whatever thoughts she had about the situation she kept to herself.

"The mon is two houses down," Duncan said as they stopped again in front of the nun's home. He helped Elsbeth down, and they walked to a small, dilapidated structure that Duncan would be hard pressed to call a house. He looked around, and it seemed to be the only place Darby could be.

He stepped up and knocked on the door.

"Whoe'er ye are, go away, unless yer bringing some good Scottish whisky."

They grinned at each other. Duncan shouted, "Darby. This is Laird Duncan Grant from Clan Grant. I need to speak with ye."

After a few minutes, the door creaked open. Darby had to be at least one hundred years. He was bent over, wrinkled, and leaned on a cane. His ragged kilt almost dragged on the floor, and his bonnet had seen many years—and few washings. "What do ye want with me, Laird?"

"We are looking for information on the nuns who live over there." He gestured in the direction of the large building on the corner.

His demeanor changed to one of suspicion. "What do ye want with them?"

Elsbeth said before Duncan could reply, "I was to join them today, but there is no one there. Yet, it looks as though the place is being used."

Darby sighed. "'Tis a sad story, my lady." He backed up and waved them in. If ye care to join me for a bit, I'll tell ye what happened."

Amazingly enough, the inside of the small house was clean and well kept. 'Twas apparent the man liked his whisky with the two empty jugs sitting on the table.

Once they all sat on the benches at the rough-hewn table, he leaned forward and said, "They were arrested."

Elsbeth gasped. "Why?"

Darby slammed his cane on the floor. "'Tis that blasted Charles!" He looked over at Elsbeth. "Pardon my language, my lady."

"The king?" Duncan asked.

"Aye. He doesn't want to bow to his mam and sister and turn Catholic. To prove how powerful and stubborn he is, he's ordered all the convents closed. I doona ken if he intended for the nuns to be arrested, but they were. The last I heard they were being sent to London."

Once more, he slammed his cane on the floor. "We need to get out from under the mon's thumb. England and its soldiers doona belong in Scotland." He waved the cane around, causing Elsbeth to duck. "Ye are a laird," he said to Duncan. "Ye need to rally the clans and fight the bloody English." He dipped his head at Elsbeth. "Again, my apologies, my lady."

"When did this happen?" Duncan asked.

"Just two days past."

Duncan had no idea what Elsbeth thought of the whole thing. Most likely she was stunned. "Thank ye, Darby. If ye would join us at the public house later, I'll see that ye have a few cups of whisky for yer trouble."

The man grinned. "Aye. I will be there." He winked. "And mayhap a meat pie or two?"

As they stood to leave, Darby said, "Wait. I just remembered something. Right before Sister Albert was taken away, she gave me a letter to give to a young lady who might come asking for her. She said it had arrived at the convent the week before. Might that be ye?"

"I doona ken. Is there a name on it?"

"Aye. Let me get it for ye." The old man hobbled to the back of the room and picked up a letter, sealed with a stamp. He handed it to her.

"It says Lady Elsbeth Johnstone," Elsbeth said.

"Is that ye?"

"Aye." Elsbeth frowned as she studied the seal for a few moments and looked at Duncan. "'Tis from my da."

"How verra strange. How would he ken to send ye a letter here?"

Elsbeth broke the seal on the missive and shrugged. "I sent him a letter before I left Dornoch telling him I was travelling to Perth to join the sisters."

Her eyes skimmed over the note, and she turned a ghastly shade of white. "He's on his way here."

"What?"

Her eyes moved back and forth as she skimmed the note again. "He says I am not to take any vows, and he is on his way, but he's not alone." She looked up at him.

"Who is with him?"

Elsbeth swallowed. A few times. "My betrothed."

10

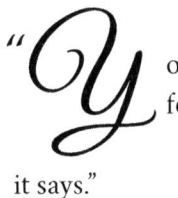

"Your betrothed!" Duncan shouted loud enough for both Darby and Elsbeth to jump.

Elsbeth looked at the note again. "'Tis what it says."

For probably the first time in his life, Duncan was truly speechless. *Her betrothed?* How is it a woman who is preparing to take a nun's vows is promised to a man?

He turned and walked a few steps away, running his fingers through his hair. He turned back and studied a very surprised-looking Elsbeth. "Can ye explain that to me, lass?"

Slowly, she lowered the paper and looked over at him. "I doona think so. I have no idea." She waved the paper around. "This is quite the surprise."

Darby—the old fool—cackled like a chicken and slapped his thigh. "This sounds like a real story, my laird."

Duncan took a deep breath. "Does it say when he expects to arrive?"

"Nay. Only that I was to stay here and no' take vows."

Feeling a bit frantic as well as confused, he said, "Obviously, ye canna stay here. I willna allow it." He paced for a few minutes. "We will return to the public house." He looked in old Darby's direction. It just occurred to him that with the nuns gone, Darby was most likely without the means to eat. Even with everything else on his mind, he couldna leave the old man to his own care.

"Darby, can ye ride a horse?"

The little man drew himself up, pushing his wee chest out. "Of course, I can ride. What sort of a mon do ye think I am?"

Hiding his smile, Duncan said, "Then I suggest when ye come to the public house later, ye bring yer things with ye. I doona think ye can stay here with the nuns gone."

Although he looked as though his pride wanted to refute Duncan's statement, the man nodded. "Aye. 'Tis a bit hungry I am."

"Do ye have a horse?"

Old Darby shook his head. "Nay. I can hardly feed myself."

"Pack yer things. Ye can ride Lady Elsbeth's horse, and she will ride with me."

A very strong finger poked him in the back as the man shuffled off to gather his few belongings. "Who gives ye the right to offer my horse to someone? And why did ye say ye wouldna allow me to stay here? And when did ye become the mon to direct my life?"

"The minute ye stepped into my castle, I became yer laird. And it remains so until ye are settled under another chieftain."

Her voice lowered, and her jaw tightened. "I was

dragged away from my group and forced to yer castle. How does that make ye my laird?"

"Elsbeth, ye are being unreasonable. Ye kenned all yer life how things are for women, whether ye like it or no'. Ye need a mon to protect ye—"

"—protection doesn't mean telling me what to do, where to go, where no' to go, and who can ride my horse."

"If ye are both finished shouting at each other, I'm ready to leave, Laird." Old Darby stood clutching a small cloth bag. "'Tis a good thing my hearing isna what it used to be." He shook his head and moved past them to the door. He turned back "Are ye coming?"

Duncan stormed to the door and directed the old man to Elsbeth's horse. "Ye can ride that one."

Despite her scowl, Elsbeth moved to his horse and attempted to mount. He walked behind her, placed his hands on her waist, and hoisted her onto the saddle. Within a flash, he was behind her, his arms wrapped around her warm body.

"Ach. I better leave a note for my da," Elsbeth said, attempting to wiggle from his arms.

"I'll do it. Ye stay here." Duncan jumped from the horse again. "Since there were nuns living inside, I assume there will be some paper and a writing instrument. I will be but a moment."

A riffle through what must have been Sister Albert's desk turned up a few sheets of parchment, a quill, and an inkpot. He wrote to Laird Johnstone that his daughter was at the public house at the north end of Perth.

Hoping the weather stayed dry, he left the letter on the front step of the building with a heavy rock holding it down.

Once he was back on the horse, he nudged the animal with his knees and they set off, with old Darby behind them, chuckling again.

* * *

Elsbeth's emotions were so tumbled 'twas a wonder she didn't begin screaming and pulling out her hair. It had been her choice to join a convent. The convent was empty, the nuns arrested. Her da was coming to keep her from joining even if the nuns were still there.

The most terrifying part of the entire disaster was her da bringing her betrothed. Christ's toes! A betrothed. Who the devil was this man?

She knew there had been no betrothal when she left her da's home to travel back to Dornoch. Or even any talk of it. No correspondence from him followed that he was arranging such a thing. 'Twas no wonder she shouted at Duncan.

She sighed.

"Lay yer head back on my chest. With how stiff ye are holding yerself, yer headache will soon return." Duncan's soft, soothing voice edged the tears she'd been holding back a bit closer.

She sniffed but refused to cry. "My headache, Laird, is sitting behind me."

Although she wasn't in a humorous state of mind, she was forced to smile when Duncan threw his head back and laughed. "Ach, lass, ye are funny even when ye doona intend to be."

Taking his advice, she leaned against his chest. His

warm, hard, powerful chest. He wanted to protect her, comfort her, which she understood having watched Conall and Haydon, but he wasn't her husband. Nor her laird. Nor her brother, or da. He had no intention of declaring himself, so why did she feel this sense of safety when with him? And by what right did he act as her keeper?

'Twas a short ride, and once they left the horses behind in the stable, and old Darby was off to the public house with permission to put his meal and drinks on Duncan's bill, Elsbeth took in a deep breath and turned to him. "I doona wish to return to the room again. I have quite a bit to think about."

Duncan nodded. "I understand, lass, but where do ye intend to do yer thinking?"

"I just wish to take a walk. Fresh air will clear my head." 'Twas not the best of weather, since the air had turned cooler, and given the gathering of clouds in the distance, she could be soaking wet upon her return.

Duncan placed his hands behind his back and regarded her. "I doona want to sound like a tyrant again, but I canna allow ye to wander around a strange town by yerself."

His words, of course, were no surprise. Even though he filled no formal part of her life, he would be expected to keep her safe. "Aye. I understand, but I'm no' in the mood for company."

He studied her for a moment, then shrugged. "'Tis no' a problem. I will walk alongside ye but will not speak."

She gave a curt nod and began her stroll. Which turned into more of a march, but Duncan kept up with her. After about ten minutes during which she dinna spend any time thinking of her issues, the nearness of Duncan taking up her space and thoughts, he said, "Do ye want to talk about it, lass?"

She whirled around. "About what? The appalling decision I made? The convent closed up, the nuns gone? Or my da coming to fetch me like a bairn? Or suddenly being faced with a betrothal to someone I doona even ken? Or—nay, ne'er mind." She looked at him, feeling as though this was the only person in the world who could keep her from crumbling into an emotional mess.

Duncan reached out and touched her cheek. "Ah, lass. 'Tis a sorry state for ye, to be sure. What say ye we go closer to the town and mayhap find a crofter or two whose work ye can admire? Instead of thinking about all yer troubles, forget them for a while."

"Aye."

He took her arm and they walked at a more sedate pace. She immediately felt a sense of calm come over her. 'Twas probably the best idea to push it all aside for a few hours. Fretting was not going to change things.

Her da was coming with a betrothal. She, of course, would not accept it. Even if the man was the handsomest, kindest, wealthiest man in the Highlands. She'd turned down Duncan with all his qualities because he didn't love her.

Although she feared she was halfway—or more—in love with him.

She gave a soft laugh and shook her head at where her thoughts had wandered. She just got through telling herself she would push it all to the back of her mind.

'Twas time to take her own advice. "What I need, Laird, is a good chess game."

His eyes grew warm as he studied her. "Do ye think ye could concentrate on it right now, lass?"

"I willna ken unless I try."

"Come," he tugged her toward an alehouse across the road. "Oftentimes these places have various games to keep drinkers refilling their cups. I have no way of kenning if they have chess, but there would be some sort of game that might take yer mind off yer troubles."

The building appeared newer than the others they'd passed. The inside was dim and smelled of whisky and ale. Duncan led her to a table, and they sat across from each other on the hard benches.

A young serving maid approached them. One look at Duncan from across the room, and her hips began to sway. The tart licked her lips and shifted her bodice to reveal a bit more skin.

Elsbeth wanted to slap her.

"Good afternoon, sir. What can I get for ye?"

"Ye are speaking to the Laird of Clan Grant, lass," Elsbeth said in a very precise manner. She was not going to have this wench falling all over Duncan.

Instead of looking abashed, the serving maid smiled even brighter. "Is that so? Well, good afternoon, Laird." She dipped, revealing a bit more of her bosom.

Duncan looked at Elsbeth, from the humor in his eyes he knew she was annoyed at the lass's attention. "Are ye hungry, my dear?"

"Nay. A cup of ale would be fine." She nudged him. "And a chess board."

"Chess?" the lass asked, looking back and forth between them.

"Do ye have one?" Duncan asked.

She frowned. "No one e'er asked for one before. I can ask Marley. He's the owner." She began to walk away and came back. "'Tis a game, right?"

"Aye. And I'll have a cup of ale also."

"Oh, sorry my laird. I guess I forgot to ask ye." She walked off, her hips swaying so enthusiastically, Elsbeth expected her to bump into one of the tables and knock a drink to the floor.

"I doona think we'll find a chess game here," Elsbeth said as she looked around the room. "'Tis doubtful any of them ken the game."

Duncan scanned the place as well. "It seems there are more than a few serious drinkers here. If we are unable to get the game, we will enjoy our ale and return to the public house."

"They have a chess game there?"

Duncan shrugged. "I doona ken, but I brought mine with me."

Elsbeth's spirits lifted, and a warm feeling surrounded her. "Aye. Verra good, Laird. I think I would prefer to use yer set even if they have one here."

"So ye are back to calling me Laird again? I thought we decided on Duncan."

Before she could respond, the serving lass returned with two cups of ale that she placed in front of them. "I'm verra sorry, Laird, but we doona have a chess set."

Duncan lifted his ale. "'Tis all right, lass."

She leaned closer to him and smiled. "Is there anything else I can do for ye?" She glanced in Elsbeth's direction and smirked, lowering her voice, although loud enough that Elsbeth heard every disgusting word. "Something yer wife willna do?" Her tongue slowly ran around her lips. "Her being a lady and all."

Elsbeth stood and tossed her ale into the lass's face. Shocked at her actions, she swept her skirts away from the table and left the alehouse. She'd only gone a few steps when Duncan jogged up alongside her. "Well done, lass."

"Ach, the wench is lucky I dinna pull all her hair out too."

With a chuckle, Duncan took her arm and steered her toward the public house. "Time for a nice, relaxing game of chess, my lady."

* * *

THE PUBLIC HOUSE WAS QUIET. Most of the men who did their drinking there were most likely busy doing whatever it was they did to provide for their families.

Duncan's men were nowhere in sight, but old Darby sat at one of the tables in the rear of the room. He offered them a huge smile and held up his ale cup. "Thank ye, my laird."

Duncan nodded and headed in his direction. "Did ye get yer meat pie?"

"Aye. Two of them." The little man rubbed his stomach. "If ye doona mind, my laird, the innkeeper said I could bed down with yer men in the stable."

"'Twould be fine. Lady Elsbeth and I are going to play a game of chess. Do ye want to join us?" He hoped the man would say no, since 'twould be hard to concentrate with the old man watching them.

"Nay. Thank ye, but I'm happy just sitting here enjoying my ale." He raised his cup again, and Duncan walked back to the table where Elsbeth sat.

Just then Darby began to sing an old Scottish song, waving his cup back and forth.

"Ach. I doona think we'll be able to concentrate on the game here either," Elsbeth said. She thought for a moment. "We can set up the game in my room upstairs."

Duncan's first reaction was to suggest that was not smart. Him and Elsbeth in her bedroom? Dangerous plan. Therefore, he was surprised to hear himself say, "Aye, lass. That's a good idea."

He fetched his chess board and pieces from the bag in the stable. He found his men there cheering each other in a game of knucklebones. Old Darby was still singing away when Duncan passed through the main room.

Elsbeth had spread a blanket on the floor of her room. The only other space they would have been able to play was on the bed, so the lass had made a good choice.

They set up the chess board and soon were deep in the game. He studied her while she chewed her lip and thought about her moves. The sun shone through the window, casting her red curls into ringlets of fire. Lady Elsbeth Johnstone was a beautiful woman who he'd desired from the time she elbowed him in his stomach and butted his chin with her head as they wrestled on his horse after they took her from her escort.

There were so many parts to this woman. She was soft, caring, and helpful. She could be a firebrand when she wished and sultry when she felt the same desire he did.

He would do almost anything to have her as his wife.

Except promise her love.

She leaned over the board, apparently paying closer attention to the game than he had. Moving her knight, she grinned at him and declared "Checkmate."

He didn't look at the board but continued to look at her face as she broke out into a triumphant smile. He reached out and cupped her head with his hands. "Ye are so beautiful, Elsbeth. Ye take my breath away."

He rubbed his thumbs over her soft cheeks. "Yer skin is soft like a rose petal."

She wrapped her hands around his wrists, leaning her face into his hand, rubbing her cheek against his palm.

Unable to stop himself, Duncan shifted his hands to her shoulders and drew her across the board, scattering pieces as he wrapped his arms around her and pulled her flush against his chest.

Her mouth was heaven. Soft, warm, moist. She smelled of summer and fresh air. She slid her hands up his chest to encircle his neck. Her slight moan brought him to the edge.

The entire time he was more than aware of the bed only a few steps away from them. A nice, soft bed where he could lay her down and introduce her to passion. Teach her the ways they could pleasure each other.

His fingers, busy loosening her plait, felt stiff and awkward. What he wanted the clumsy things to do was loosen her bodice, revealing her lush breasts to him. Once he released her hair, she shook her head, and the beautiful locks tumbled down her back. He fisted the silky strands and pulled her head back and placed soft kisses on her neck, throat, and along her collarbone.

He swept away the chess pieces and laid them both down. His now less than stiff fingers undid her bodice and spread the garment apart. His knuckle circled her stiff nipple, and she moaned again.

"Where is Lady Elsbeth Johnstone!" A very, very loud

voice echoed up from the main floor. "Daughter, ye better present yerself. Posthaste!"

Her face pale, her eyes wide, Elsbeth yanked herself away from him, quickly lacing up her bodice. She jumped up, started to plait her hair, then shrugged and hurried to the door.

Still lying on the floor, elbow bent, his hand propping up his head, he smiled and said, "I assume yer da has arrived?"

11

*E*lsbeth flew down the stairs to where Da waited at the bottom, scowling at her. "Daughter, ye will find someplace we can talk in private."

Trying to catch her breath and calm her pounding heart, she said. "Good day to ye, Da. 'Tis nice to see ye too."

Looking a bit abashed, he said, "Good day to ye as well." He stepped up and offered her a kiss on the cheek. He moved back and pointed his finger at her. "Now find someplace we can talk in private."

God's bones! Duncan was in her room so she couldna bring him there. She fumbled for a few moments until the sound of footsteps coming down the stairs calmed her a bit. She sighed with relief when Duncan came to stand alongside her.

He bowed at her da. "Good afternoon. I assume ye are Laird Johnstone of the Johnstone Clan?" Duncan looked everything a powerful laird should be. His attitude was open and friendly, with steel in his eyes.

Da's eyes narrowed. "Aye. And who ye be?"

Duncan stuck his arm out. "I am Duncan Grant, Laird of the Clan Grant."

Her da stared at Duncan's outstretched hand and reluctantly took it, giving a quick shake. He turned back to Elsbeth. "Do ye ken this mon?"

"Aye, Da. He and his men escorted me to the convent."

He looked back and forth between the two of them. "The Laird of Clan Grant escorted ye from Dornoch?"

"Not precisely." The pounding of her heart started up again. "But it's a bit of a story."

Da nodded. "I will hear the tale." He looked over at Duncan. "Thank ye for seeing my daughter safely arrived. Ye can leave now, she is under the protection of her betrothed."

Duncan and Elsbeth both looked over Da's shoulder to the man she hadn't noticed until now. He was not as tall as Duncan. Not as braw as Duncan. Not as handsome as Duncan. Brown eyes instead of hazel like Duncan's.

He stepped forward and bowed. "My lady. 'Tis a pleasure to meet my future wife. I am William MacMillan of the MacMillan Clan." His chest stuck out as he gazed at her, his chin tilted up, looking down his nose at her.

She gave a quick dip and turned to her da. "Da. There is something we need to discuss." She looked over at MacMillan again. "Now."

"There is time to discuss everything later. 'Tis sure I am ye will be pleased with the match and what it will bring to ye and our clan." He looked once more at Duncan. "Again, I thank ye, laird, but ye and yer men can depart now." He scratched his head. "Although I would like to ken how ye came to escort my daughter from Dornoch."

She had to get control of the situation. If she thought before now that she wouldn't marry this man her da had betrothed her to, after meeting him there was absolutely no chance of that occurring.

Duncan stepped forward. "My men and I will be here for a bit, Laird. May I suggest we all take a seat at one of the tables and have a bite to eat and some whisky or ale to relax ye and MacMillan after yer journey?"

Da seemed taken aback by Duncan's blunt words, but she knew Duncan would not be easily dismissed. Now that she'd gotten over the shock of her da standing here in front of her, with this unacceptable man leering at her breasts, her mind wandered back to the kiss she and Duncan had shared. She couldna help but wonder how far things would have gone had her da not interrupted them. Hopefully, the blush she felt rising to her face would be attributed to her race down the stairs.

"Aye, Laird," Da said, "'tis probably a good idea to have some food and drink. Will ye be joining us?"

"Without a doubt, Laird," Duncan responded. Taking charge, he walked them to one of the tables. A few others had filled up. The customers eyed their group curiously, but then went back to their meal.

The young maid who had served them since they'd arrived approached their table. "Good eve, Laird, my lady."

"Good eve, lass. What is the special in the kitchen today?" Elsbeth asked.

"Mutton stew, and Mrs. McDonough's fresh bread."

Elsbeth smiled, her stomach rumbling despite the hardships and surprises of the day. "I will have that, and a cup of ale, please." The lass took everyone else's order which mimicked Elsbeth's.

William leaned forward and covered Elsbeth's hand with his. Sweaty. Slimy. She tried very hard not to shiver. "Ye are everything yer da said. And more. Ye are quite pleasing to the eye, and yer da tells me ye are quite calm and even-tempered unlike yer sister who is no' so agreeable."

Slowly, Elsbeth inched her hand back, barely stopping from wiping it on her dress. "My sister's husband, Laird Haydon Sutherland, finds Ainslee quite agreeable, Mr. MacMillan."

The fool man smirked at her as if she were not in on a secret only he knew. Aye, the man certainly made her skin crawl.

Things remained quiet at the table. Once the ale had been placed before them, along with the stew bowls, bread, and freshly churned butter, da looked at Elsbeth in a manner that had her shifting in her chair like a bairn.

"I want to ken why The Sutherland permitted ye to believe it would be acceptable to join a convent?"

"Foolish idea," Mr. MacMillan said, patting her hand once again. She moved the hand she wasn't eating with to her lap.

"I felt helping Sister Albert with her work would be the best thing for me. It did take some persuasion, but Haydon finally relented."

Da pointed a buttered piece of bread at her. "And hearing from me he will be, allowing ye to do something so reckless." He shook his head and shoved the bread into his mouth.

Once again MacMillan opened his mouth, his demeanor one of chastising a young lass. "'Ye are far too beautiful to be hidden away in a convent." He shook his head, his lips pursed as he stared at her breasts. "I willna have any problem getting bairns on ye."

Dumping her stew over the idiot man's head would not be as forgiven as tossing ale in the server's face earlier, but unable to bear another minute of this man's presence, she hopped up from her seat. "If ye will excuse me, I feel my headache returning. I shall retire for the night."

Da rose. "Nay, daughter. We will speak as soon as the meal is finished, headache or no."

She raised her chin, reclaimed her seat, and turned to Duncan. So far, she had found Mr. MacMillan and her da unbearable. 'Twas now his turn. "Nothing to say, my laird?"

His words, "Nay, lass," offered very little, but his tightened lips and the anger in his eyes told her a lot more than the other two men knew.

Truth be told, Duncan's presence and strength kept her from saying something that would shame her da and probably cause him to drag her back to Lochwood Tower by her hair.

MacMillan slurping his food and grunting every time he shoveled the stew into his mouth became the next thing she found insufferable. Was her da growing decrepit in his old age? Surely, he didn't think she would marry this unmannered oaf. Or was this to be her punishment for switching places with Ainslee?

* * *

DUNCAN RETURNED his eating dagger to his belt and cleared his throat to gain Johnstone's attention.

MacMillan was picking his teeth with his dirty fingernail and had already belched a few times. 'Twas obvious

Elsbeth had no use for the man, which would make his meeting with Laird Johnstone easier.

"Laird, I would speak with ye. In private."

The old laird studied him for a minute. Glanced back and forth between him and Elsbeth. "Aye."

They both stood. "I think a walk around outside would be good for the digestion," Duncan said. He had no idea how the laird was going to take his words and preferred to not have Elsbeth and her supposed betrothed hear them.

The two men left the building and walked about thirty feet when Johnstone turned to him. "I'm trying my best, Laird, to think good things about ye and my daughter." He crossed his arms over his chest. "But I'm pondering ye might have something to say to me that I'm no' going to like."

Duncan shrugged. "I see no reason for ye not to like what I have to say. I am asking yer permission to marry yer daughter."

Johnstone waved his hand and turned to walk back to the building. "Nay. She's already betrothed."

"If ye will listen for a minute, Laird," he shouted.

The man turned and walked back. "What I would like to listen to is why you, from Clan Grant, escorted my daughter who was living with her sister in the Sutherland Clan, to Perth? Seems a tad out of yer way to fetch her from Dornoch."

How much to tell the man? If he admitted stealing the lass away from her group, he had strong doubts it would increase the man's likelihood of allowing his request to marry Elsbeth.

"Lady Elsbeth ended up at my castle due to a case of mistaken identity. We meant her no harm, and she stayed with us until the weather was clear enough for me and my men to escort her to Perth to the convent."

The man's eyes narrowed, and he pulled himself up to his full height. He waved a finger in Duncan's face. "Are ye asking for the lass's hand because after staying with ye, she is no longer a maid? No longer possesses her virtue?" His face grew red, and his voice rose on the last few words to the point that Duncan felt Elsbeth and MacMillan probably did hear them inside the building.

"Nay, Laird. Yer daughter remains untouched. While at my castle, she was under my protection. As an honorable mon, I would ne'er allow anything like that to happen."

'Twas wise to forget how close they came to discarding that virtue right before the lass's da had arrived. At least now, he could face the man and tell him his daughter was untouched without guilt.

"As to yer request, the answer is nay," the older laird groused, "I made an arrangement with MacMillan, and the contracts were signed."

Duncan rocked back on his heels. "Can I ask ye, Laird, why you made an arrangement when Lady Elsbeth was headed to join a convent?"

"'Twas a stupid thing for the lass to do. She doesn't ken what she's doing most of the time. I will have a word with Sutherland about this too. Why he would allow her to do such a foolish thing needs explaining. 'Tis my fault for no' taking her in hand when she came to visit me after her sister married. I ne'er should have let her return to Dornoch." He pounded his fist in his hand. "'Tis the lass's duty to marry and marry who I say."

"Then you believe yer daughter has no say in who she marries?"

"Why should she? Her sister married the mon I made a contract with."

Duncan decided if he had any chance of changing the laird's mind, it would not be a good idea to remind him that the daughter he'd made the contract for switched places with her twin.

"Can I ask a favor of ye, then, Johnstone?" Duncan asked. He had to think fast because this man was not budging, and even if he never talked Elsbeth into marrying him, he knew she would be miserable the rest of her life with MacMillan. That he would not allow. He cared too much for the lass.

But not enough to love her?

"What?" Johnstone said.

"Give me a few days to change yer mind." He held up his hand when the laird opened his mouth to speak. "As one laird to another. I doona see any reason to rush this. I think yer daughter would be a happier wife if she felt she had some say in who she married."

The man stared at him for much too long for his comfort. "I need to speak with my daughter. I'm no' saying that will change my mind, but I haven't seen her in a while." He hung his head, then looked back up at him, his eyes misty. "It may not seem so to ye, but I love my lasses. I only want what's best for them. 'Tis my duty as their da to see them settled and happy with their own homes, husband, and bairns."

All the bad feelings Duncan had garnered for Johnstone melted away like butter in the sun. "I agree with ye," Duncan said. "When the time comes for me to deal with grown up lasses of my own, I intend to take my responsibilities seriously also."

Johnstone slapped him on the back. "Let's go have

another ale or two, Laird, and mayhap in the morning we can hash this all out."

Once they reached the door, Johnstone turned and said, "But I'll no' be changing my mind about the marriage contract. She *will* marry MacMillan."

12

*E*lsbeth tossed and turned in her bed. She pounded the pillow into submission, then tossed and turned some more.

She flipped onto her back, lacing her fingers together over her stomach, staring at the canopy. Finally with a deep sigh, she threw the bedcovers off and stood. Even though 'twas summer, the air was chilly in the room, and her feet were icy on the stone floor.

A full moon lit the room as bright as daylight and drew her to the window. She leaned her elbows on the window frame, and resting her chin on her hands, she stared at the stable no more than a quarter mile behind the public house, cast in an eerie glow.

Duncan was in there. Asleep.

She paced.

Da had not given her the chance to talk to Duncan once the two men had returned from their walk. Neither one had looked happy, and she couldna guess what that meant.

As soon as they'd reached her table, Da had held out his hand. "I will escort ye to yer room, daughter. Where I expect ye to be when I return in the morning to escort ye to break yer fast." He'd frowned at Duncan. "Where are ye sleeping, Laird?"

Duncan had looked offended, his eyes flashing and his chin lifted. "In the stable with my men. That's where I've been since we arrived."

Da had granted him an abrupt nod. "See that ye stay there."

She'd panicked for a moment when Duncan had reached for his sword, but her whispered, 'please,' stopped him.

Mr. MacMillan had then stood. "Laird, I believe I should sleep in front of the lass's door for the night."

Duncan had reached for his sword again, but this time had it partially out when it looked as though Da was considering such a thing.

"Nay," she'd said. "I willna be treated like a prisoner."

"The lass is right, MacMillan. Ye will sleep in the room I secured for the two of us."

Duncan's sword had slid back in.

Now as she continued to pace and try to quell the anger at this entire mess, she knew no matter what became of her decision, she had to speak with Duncan. She needed to know what he and Da had talked about. 'Twas her life, and she was mighty tired of everyone making decisions for her. Of men talking about her behind her back. Treating her like a bairn, making arrangements about her life without her knowledge.

Ainslee had taken her future into her own hands when she stepped into Elsbeth's place at the wedding. They were twins, of the same blood. 'Tis time she shed her 'very nice lass' attitude and took on more of her sister's behavior.

She threw her arisaidh over her shoulders, laced up her boots, and left the room. The inn was quiet and dark which told her it was quite late, the skittering of small nighttime animals the only sound. She stepped out of the building and headed toward the stables. Thankfully, the full moon lit her way, keeping her from stumbling over rocks and branches.

Once she reached the stable, she stood with her hands on her hips, staring at the building. Now that she was there, how was she to get Duncan's attention when he was most likely sleeping alongside his men.

She chewed on her lip for a minute, then slowly opened the stable door flinching at every squeak the door made. She gasped and stepped back as the door seemed to open on its own.

"What are ye doing, lass?" Duncan whispered and stepped out to join her.

He was fully dressed, his hair a mess from running his fingers through it. It appeared he'd had no more sleep than her. "Christ's toes, Duncan, ye scared me to death." She placed her hand over her pounding heart. "What are ye doing up?"

He took her arm and walked her about twenty steps from the door. "Most likely the same thing ye are doing up. I canna sleep."

"Aye, me neither." She shivered, the arisaidh not keeping her particularly warm. "I wanted to ken what ye and my da talked about," she whispered.

He hesitated for a moment. "I asked him for yer hand in marriage."

Her brows rose almost to her hairline. "Indeed? And why would ye do that when I told ye before I will only marry for love."

"Are ye telling me ye love MacMillan?"

She dismissed his words as nonsense with a flick of her hand. "Of course no'. I have no intention of marrying that noxious oaf."

"Well, yer da seems to think ye will do just that. As does MacMillan."

"What did my da say to your proposal?" 'Twas a silly question because if Da had said yes, he would have told her when they'd returned instead of threatening Duncan about staying away from her all night.

"He said precisely what I expected him to say. Nay. He is determined ye will honor the contract he signed with MacMillan."

Elsbeth poked her finger in his chest. "The time has ended for everyone telling me what to do. I am pulled this way, and then that way, and told to do this, and told to do that."

Duncan tugged her farther from the stable. "Calm down, lass, or ye will wake everyone in the stable and the public house."

She dashed her palm over her cheeks to wipe the tears that had started. If she couldna keep herself from falling apart, she would never convince all these men that she was a strong lass who could decide for herself how to conduct her life.

Duncan tucked a curl blowing in the light breeze behind her ear. "Doona fash yerself, Elsbeth. I will take care of this for ye. Trust me."

She raised her chin, adopting a cool, almost noble stance. "Ye have no' been listening to me. I will no longer allow men to decide my future, or to solve my problems. I doona care if that is the way of the world. 'Twill no longer be the way of my world.

"Now, I will bid ye good night, Laird." She turned on her heel and strode away. The sound of Duncan following behind her to the door of the public house comforted her, even though she was mad at every man who walked the earth.

Still not tired enough to sleep, she spent some time pondering what to do when the sun rose, and she had to face three men who all thought they knew what was best for her.

Pfft. She was the one who knew what was best for her. And that was to decide how she wanted to conduct the rest of her life. Because of the way things were for women, she still needed a man's protection and support, but she would find that at Dornoch Castle.

When she returned, she would find her place there. She'd spent far too much time feeling sorry for herself, especially after Conall married and she saw how perfect he and Maura were together. She didn't have to be married to be fulfilled. This time when she arrived at Dornoch, it would be as a strong, confident woman.

In the morn, she would tell her da of her decision. Unless he planned to tie her up and drag her back to Lochwood Tower, he would not get his way. Neither would MacMillan. Nor Duncan.

With thought, she was finally able to fall asleep.

With a smile on her face.

* * *

THE NEXT MORN, Duncan arrived in the public house main room. 'Twas early, but Laird Johnstone, MacMillan, and Elsbeth were all seated at a table. They sipped on ale, and no one spoke. He joined them and wished them all a good morn.

There were mumbled responses. "Now that ye are all here, I have an announcement to make," Elsbeth said.

Three men folded their arms across their chests, leaning back in their chairs and glaring at her. Before she could speak, old Darby wandered into the room. "Good morn! I see ye are all ready to break yer fast. I'll be happy to join ye."

Without an invitation, he pulled up a chair and rubbed his hands together. "I'm for some sausages and eggs."

Duncan took a deep breath. "What is it ye want to say, Elsbeth?" He didn't like the look on her face. She appeared determined, as if ready for a fight.

"She is Lady Elsbeth to ye," MacMillan said. Duncan opened his mouth as she held up her hand. "Doona distract me. I have something to say, and I want ye all to hear it."

Darby smiled. "I like ye lass. 'Tis good to be a strong woman." He reached over and took the cup of ale in front of Elsbeth and took a gulp. He waved his hand "Go on, lass."

She nodded in his direction. "Today I am leaving Perth and traveling to Dornoch Castle where I will take up permanent residence."

The shouting in the room drowned out old Darby's cackling. He slapped his thigh and thumped his cane. "That's it, lassie. Tell them what ye are to do." He looked around and waved at the serving lass who entered the room. Most likely to see what all the noise was about.

Once again, Elsbeth held up her hand. "I will allow each of ye to speak. In turn."

"What are ye about, daughter? I doona need permission to speak," the laird shouted.

"Yes. Ye do. I am tired of everyone telling me what to do. What not to do. I ken it's an unusual thing for a woman to have a say over her life, but my sister did it, and I intend to do the same." She sat back, her arms crossed underneath her bosom.

Silence. The serving maid looked at each of them, her face pale. "Are ye all wanting sausages and eggs? Warm bread as well?"

"Aye, bring it all," MacMillan said. "Some oatcakes, too." Apparently, nothing that had happened so far had deprived him of his appetite.

Johnstone banged his fist on the table. "Ye are my daughter, and I insist ye honor the marriage contract I signed for ye."

Instead of arguing or getting angry, Elsbeth merely smiled and said, "Nay."

Duncan would have cheered except he had a feeling he wasn't going to like what she said next. Almost as if she read his mind, she turned to him. "I will no' be marrying anyone. No' unless I decide 'tis what I want. And ye ken what that is, Laird Grant."

"Now just a minute," MacMillan said. "Ye are betrothed to me, and I insist ye honor the betrothal contract. 'Tis the best thing for the MacMillan clan and the Johnstone clan."

The lass leaned forward. "If ye want an alliance between clans, I suggest ye find someone else to marry." She glanced at her da who watched her with shock.

Once again, Johnstone slammed his fist on the table, his

eyes ablaze. "This is an abomination! Enough of this nonsense, daughter! Ye will do as ye are told."

"Nay." She thanked the serving girl who placed food in the center of the table and trenchers for them to fill. Then the lass hurried away, no doubt not wanting to get involved in the very loud argument.

MacMillan began to fill his trencher. "Ye will honor the contract, lass, even if I have to force ye there."

Duncan stood and leaned into MacMillan's face. "If ye put so much as a finger on her, ye will find yerself tasting the stone floor."

"These are verra good sausages, eh?" Darby said.

"I have a signed contract with the laird. Legal," MacMillan mumbled, the food in his mouth sliding down his chin.

Elsbeth smiled sweetly at MacMillan. "Then marry *him.*"

"Blasphemy Daughter!" Duncan thought the laird's head was going to explode. "I ne'er heard ye speak like this." He turned his attention to Duncan and waved his eating dagger at him. "This is yer fault!"

"Mine?" Duncan asked. "How do ye figure that?"

"Elsbeth has always been a sweet, obedient lass. From the time she left the cradle, she's always done what was expected of her. 'Tis yer influence that has made her more like her sister." Johnstone banged his dagger on the table.

"Excuse me, da, but I believe ye just insulted Ainslee," Elsbeth said.

She turned to Duncan. "May I have yer permission to keep the horse you loaned me until I reach Dornoch? I will have it sent back to Freuchie."

Duncan rubbed his eyes with his index finger and

thumb. "My lady, may I have a word with ye when ye are finished?"

"Certainly." She continued to eat as if there was absolutely nothing unusual about the meal so far. He was almost as stunned as Johnstone with Elsbeth's manner. Where was the sobbing, near hysterical lass of yesterday? Not that he preferred to see her so upset, but sometime between when she left him near the stable last night and this morning, a major change had come over her.

Even though it might not bode well for him, he was quite proud of her. This new Elsbeth was even more desirable than before. He'd always knew somewhere inside her was a strong lass fighting to get out. Especially since he'd heard tales about her sister who had always been the strong one. It appeared Elsbeth learned her lessons well in watching her sister.

Elsbeth wiped her dagger clean, slid it into her belt, and stood. "Ye wished to speak with me?"

MacMillan continued to shovel food into his mouth, while Johnstone pushed his food around and glared at his daughter. Old Darby finished his meal and refilled his trencher. "Fine offerings at this place." He looked around. "I like it."

Once they were outside and a distance from the public house, he said, "What the devil is this all about, Elsbeth?"

"I assume yer hearing has started to trouble ye? I am taking my life into my own hands."

He reached out and clasped her hands in his. "Marry me, lass. I will take ye back to Freuchie where we can have a happy life."

She tilted her chin up. "Can ye promise me love?"

Duncan dropped her hands and ran his fingers through

his hair. He walked in a circle, his hands resting on his hips. "Why does it have to be love? I care for ye. I like spending time with ye. I certainly desire ye." He held his hands out in supplication. "I will provide for ye, protect ye, give ye bairns. Isna that enough?"

She sucked in a deep breath and shook her head, a soft smile on her plump lips. "I'm afraid no', Laird. I need more, and I deserve more. I want what my sister has. If I canna have a great love, I will no' marry."

"So, yer looking for a mon who is besotted with ye?"

A moment of silence. "Aye." She turned and headed back to the public house.

Why was the lass so stubborn?

Why are ye so stubborn?

* * *

ELSBETH WAS both surprised and proud of herself that she had stuck with her plan despite Da's threats to drag her before a priest, which she countered by telling him she would say 'no' when the priest presented her with the vows. And then she not-so-nicely informed MacMillan once again that under no circumstances would she marry him.

Duncan leaned against the stable doorframe, his arms crossed over his chest, his horse next to him, saddled and shaking its head restlessly, ready to go. The four men who had accompanied them from Freuchie stood nearby with their mounts. Sitting on their horses, side-by-side, Mr. MacMillan and da waited, both glowering at Duncan.

Old Darby had managed to appropriate the packhorse they'd used on their trip to Perth and seemed ready to depart the town with them. She placed her hands on her hips. "Where do ye all think ye are going?"

"Elsbeth—" Duncan started.

"Lady Elsbeth," MacMillan growled.

"—Ye canna travel by yerself. No matter how strong ye think ye are, ye are still a woman who has no' been trained in combat. I would ne'er let ye go alone. If ye are set on returning to Dornoch, I will be with ye, all the way."

"Daughter, ye will cease this nonsense right now and return with me to Lochwood Tower."

MacMillan tried to look kinder but didn't quite make it. "Lady Elsbeth, ye must honor the marriage contract, or 'twill be a disgrace for yer da."

"Are we bringing food with us, or will we be hunting? And how far is Dornoch Castle?" Darby was the last one to be heard from.

Elsbeth sighed but knew full well she couldna take the trip by herself, and also knew that neither Da nor Duncan would permit it. She wasn't stupid, after all. 'Twould be foolish and dangerous for her to insist on going alone through the wilds of the Highlands.

"If ye wish to travel with me, Laird Grant, I canna stop ye. Da, 'tis no' nonsense. 'Tis my life, and I wish to have a say. Mr. MacMillan, I believe I explained to ye already I will not be honoring the contract. My da should no' have signed it without me e'en kenning about it." She turned to the old man on the horse and offered him a smile. "I have some food with me, Darby, but I am assuming the men will be hunting if they choose to eat."

With those words, she nudged her horse and headed away from Perth. To her new life. With eight men behind her, all but Darby in a foul mood.

She smiled. 'Twas nice to have power. "I am free," she shouted. "No one will again tell me what to do."

"Elsbeth!"

She refused to turn around at Duncan's shout.

"You're going in the wrong direction, lass."

13

Duncan watched Elsbeth at the front of the group, galloping alone, wishing there was a way he could convince her to ride in the center of the escort, with the men surrounding her. 'Twas not the safest way for her to travel. Nor for the men. If they were set upon by brigands or even reivers, 'twould be hard to fight them while worrying about Elsbeth.

If she rode where she belonged, two men would immediately lead her away from any potential danger should some arise, while the others fought.

With the mood she'd been in since she first made her announcement about leaving for Dornoch, however, he thought it best to give her some time to settle down.

What he'd found interesting was the conversation between MacMillan and Johnstone. From the bits and pieces he picked up, the reason MacMillan was interested in marriage to Elsbeth was because of land and money Johnstone had promised him.

'Twas not unusual for a bride to bring a settlement with

her to the clan she married into, but in this case, the man in question seemed a bit too much determined to make the match.

As they rode along, Duncan went over in his head what he knew of the MacMillan clan. The laird was about the same age as him, having gained the lairdship a few years past. He had a younger brother breathing down his neck to be made laird. 'Twas not a situation Duncan would be happy with. Both brothers had married and both produced lasses.

'Twould be interesting to know the rank this MacMillan—William—held in the clan. Did he follow the younger brother, and was he trying to secure his place in line if there were no sons from the two men? He could do that by marrying any lass, it didn't have to be Elsbeth.

On the other hand, his insistence on the contract being honored even though 'twas obvious the bride held him in disdain could very well be a matter of a man's pride.

Neither situation meant anything to him. He would have Elsbeth for his wife. He only needed to convince her that a happy, contented marriage, without all the emotional upheaval of love would be best for her.

But she would have to come to that conclusion herself since the lass was so determined to direct her own life.

With a full breakfast, they didn't have to stop for the nooning, and only halted for those needing to relieve themselves. Johnstone took the opportunity to harass his daughter again, with MacMillan egging him on by telling him the lass should bend to her father's will, and when he married her, he would make sure she learned her place.

It took all his restraint not to pummel the obnoxious man in his face.

He decided to ask Elsbeth to go for a short walk to ease their muscles. However, MacMillan declared as his betrothed she should not be allowed to walk off with another man. After swords were partially drawn from their scabbards, Elsbeth rolled her eyes and climbed back onto her horse with Daniel's help.

Now 'twas nearing the end of the day. Johnstone had somehow maneuvered himself in front of Elsbeth, so Duncan and his men surrounded her, with MacMillan grumbling loudly at the rear. But he was much more at ease with Elsbeth being protected.

Johnstone raised his hand for them to stop. They rode off the main path, wandering into the woods for a bit to allow them protection from any surprises.

They dismounted and tended to their horses. After a walk to the small creek behind where they'd stopped, Elsbeth returned and removed a blanket from her saddle bag. Then she withdrew a bag and sauntered over to a cleared area.

She laid her items down and began to pick up small pieces of wood, ignoring the men the entire time. Duncan walked up to her. "Daniel and Gregory are going hunting."

"I have my food," she said, her cute little chin in the air.

Just like thinking she could ride all the way to Dornoch with no protection, her assumption that she could do the same with whatever food it was she had brought with her, again indicated she was not prepared for this trip, even though she thought so.

He didn't know whether to kiss her senseless or throttle her. MacMillan walked up, stood in front of Elsbeth, his feet spread apart, his hands on his hips. "This has gone on long enough, Lady Elsbeth. Ye are to return to Lochwood Tower with me and yer da tomorrow morning and prepare for yer wedding."

Duncan grinned, loving how the man was so eager to put his foot into his mouth. He merely stood and watched the anger come over Elsbeth's entire body until he thought steam would come out of her ears.

"I haven't changed my mind, Mr. MacMillan." She began to count on her fingers. "I will no' return to my da's keep tomorrow morning. I doona have a wedding to prepare for, and if I did, it wouldna be to ye."

He leaned in close to her face, and Elsbeth backed up. "When ye are my wife, ye willna be telling me what ye will and willna do. I will take great delight in teaching ye a thing or two about obedience." He smacked his fist into his palm.

Duncan stepped between them. "I warned ye already, MacMillan. Do no' even think about touching the lass. I suggest ye leave her be. She's already told ye she would not marry ye. If ye continue to harass her, ye will be answering to me."

MacMillan growled and hurled himself at Duncan. They hit the ground and fists began to fly.

* * *

"Stop this!" Elsbeth shouted, looking around frantically to have someone step in.

"Nay, lass. Let them get it out. They've been at each other since they met," her da said.

"Well, I willna stand here and watch it." She dropped the twigs she'd gathered and stomped over to where she'd placed her blanket and bag. The fight continued as old

Darby wandered over to her. "Do ye have food to share, lass?"

Although it had been her intention to let the men provide their own food, she was fond of Darby, and being an old man, he was most likely unable to hunt for himself. She smiled at him, "Aye, Darby, sit down, 'twas my intention to share with ye."

She looked over at the circle of men as they cheered the two battling men on. After a few minutes, Duncan climbed to his feet, and MacMillan lay sprawled out on the ground, knocked out. Duncan's men slapped him on the back, and he smiled.

They walked away from MacMillan and headed into the woods. Elsbeth assumed they were going to apply cold water from the creek onto Duncan's injuries.

Her da looked down at MacMillan and shook his head, then walked away. The men returned, carrying a waterskin and proceeded to dump the water onto MacMillan's head. The man came up shouting and sputtering.

"Here ye are, Darby," Elsbeth said as she handed him another piece of bread, a chunk of cheese, and an apple.

"Thank ye, lass. 'Tis grateful I am for ye sharing with me."

As she ate her food, she thought about how she'd been a bit uneasy when da took over the front of the group, afraid he would lead them all back to Lochwood Tower. Although she wasn't completely sure how to get back to Dornoch, she knew by the position of the sun before it set that they continued north.

Over the past few years, she'd ridden twice to Dornoch; when Ainslee married Haydon and when Elsbeth returned there after her visit with her da. She also traveled from there twice, including the time she'd been dragged from her tent, so she had a fair idea how to find the place.

She hadn't planned to go by herself no matter what she'd told Duncan and her da. They might be angry with her, but they were both too protective and honorable to allow her to travel alone.

"If we want to eat this eve, we better hunt our food," Duncan said to his men as they lounged on the ground, watching MacMillan stomp over to where her da sat.

"I'm no' going and leaving him," Duncan gestured to MacMillan, "alone with Lady Elsbeth. I doona trust him."

MacMillan turned to Duncan. "Aye, and I doona trust ye to be alone with Lady Elsbeth, so I'm no' going either."

Daniel, Kevin, Gregory, and John stood. "We'll do the hunting for ye."

Her da also stood. "I'll join ye."

The men all trooped off, leaving Duncan and MacMillan sitting about ten feet apart, glowering at each other. Both displaying bruised faces.

"Is no' one of ye going to make a fire? 'Twill be a chilly night and raw meat without one," Darby said as he licked his lips.

"I already gathered some twigs for ye to use," Elsbeth said, waving in the direction of the small pile she'd dropped when the fighting had begun.

Duncan stood, and MacMillan did the same. Within minutes, they had a small fire going.

"When ye are my wife, ye will share food with me. I canna believe ye sit there, feeding that old mon while yer intended husband is hungry."

"Are ye deaf, MacMillan? I doona intend to marry ye.

How many times do I have to say it before ye get it through yer thick head?"

MacMillan looked over at Duncan. "I wish to ken how ye ended up in Perth with my betrothed if she was living with her sister in Dornoch."

Elsbeth had drawn her knees up to her chest and had wrapped her arisaidh around her to stay warm. The night air had begun to grow cool. She studied Duncan as he listened to MacMillan's question.

"I believe I already answered that question to Laird Johnstone, who as her da had the right to ken."

MacMillan shifted, looking as though he was ready for another fight. "As her betrothed, I have the right to ken as well."

Duncan looked over at Elsbeth. "Lady Elsbeth, do ye remember signing a contract acknowledging a betrothal between ye and Mr. MacMillan?"

"Nay. I ne'er signed one, nor did I ever agree to one."

Duncan turned to him. "Ye see, ye have no rights where the lass is concerned."

"Her da signed the contract."

"Ah, mayhap he did, but according to Scottish law, a woman can consent to marriage by the age of twelve years. Since Lady Elsbeth is beyond that age, her consent might not be needed, but it is certainly considered."

MacMillan stood. "The mon is always in charge."

"Ye think so, Mr. MacMillan," Elsbeth asked. "There are clans in Scotland where the direct line for the laird to inherit is a woman. Men are no' always in charge."

"No' yer clan!"

Just then the men returned, carrying three rabbits and two plump pigeons. Hopefully, Duncan and MacMillan would be too busy cleaning, cooking, and eating to fight again.

Once the men had eaten their meal, Duncan stood and walked over to where Elsbeth and Darby chatted away. The old man was certainly entertaining. She was quite sure Haydon would welcome him since he had nowhere to seek food with the nuns gone.

Duncan held his hand out. "Would ye care for a stroll before sleep?"

Her heart fluttered at his look and touch as she took his hand. His poor handsome face was a bit battered, but he was still a fine-looking man. "Aye."

"Nay," MacMillan growled from the other side of the fire. "Ye willna be taking a stroll with my betrothed."

Once on her feet, Elsbeth stomped over to where her da sat, looking as though he was ready for sleep. "Da."

He looked up at her and straightened. "What is it lass?"

"I refuse to acknowledge Mr. MacMillan as my betrothed. Ye need to tell him the contract is broken."

"I'm afraid I canna do that, lass."

She placed her hands on her hips. "And why no'?"

He climbed to his feet and ran his palm down his face. "The contract was a three-way agreement."

She frowned. "Three-way? What nonsense is this?"

"The arrangement was between MacMillan, me, and his laird."

Duncan had joined her and glared at her da. "There is no such thing."

"Nay, Laird. A contract can be whate'er ye want it to be. MacMillan's laird approached me about an alliance between them and my clan. I agreed since 'twas past the time my daughter married.

"I received a piece of land that backs up to my land. We made a promise between us to provide warriors and horses in case of an attack from another clan. Mr. MacMillan received ye and his compensation, and his laird received a strip of land he wanted." He shook his head. "Even if I wanted to break the contract, I'd have to notify The MacMillan."

"'Tis a fine mess ye got me into, Da." She turned from him and walked off. "I'll be strolling by myself," she called over her shoulder.

Footsteps behind her alerted her to the fact that she wasn't alone. Two sets of footsteps told her both Duncan and MacMillan followed her.

She was beginning to feel as though she was being smothered.

* * *

Duncan had never heard of a three-party betrothal agreement. If Elsbeth's da didn't look so certain, he would have been thinking the man had made the story up. He had to admit that Johnstone did appear a tad sorry that there was the extra problem with the contract he'd signed.

Could he dare to hope the laird regretted the contract and would favor a match between him and Elsbeth? mayhap the rude way MacMillan had acted since they'd arrived in Perth had something to do with it. He knew for sure if any man talked to his daughter the way MacMillan did, there would be no marriage, no matter how difficult it was to get out of the contract.

The ground was bare in the spot they'd chosen except for where he'd set up the tent for Elsbeth. He and the other men lay near the dying fire, with John and Kevin keeping watch.

He went back over in his mind the conversation he, Elsbeth, and Laird Johnstone had about the marriage contract. While they'd been discussing it, a vague thought nudged his brain, but soon fled. Now the annoying feeling that there was something important he should remember returned to haunt him once again.

He rolled over on his back and tucked his arms behind his head. Another bright moonlit night was center stage for the millions of beautiful stars surrounding it. MacMillan's snores rattled the entire camp. There were absolutely no redeeming qualities to the man.

In a few hours, it would be his turn to take over the watch. He'd best get at least some sleep so he wasn't tumbling from his horse in a deep slumber come daylight. He closed his eyes and was just about to drift into that wonderful stage where sleep was only moments away when he sat up, his heart pounding. Words teased his brain:

"Is it possible to get a cool cloth with some lavender on it?"

"Aye. My wife surely has some. I'll send her up with it in a bit. She can help yer wife get settled."

"Is there anything else I can do for ye?" The serving lass glanced in Elsbeth's direction and smirked, lowering her voice. "Something yer wife willna do?" Her tongue slowly ran around her lips. "Her being a lady and all."

Two times during their stay in Perth, Elsbeth had been referred to as his wife. He hadn't disputed it when the innkeeper mentioned it, and neither one of them had corrected the serving lass.

There were witnesses.

According to Scottish law, they were married!

He wanted to shout the news, but then remembered something equally important. They didn't consummate the irregular marriage. Without that it wasn't considered legal. He'd already assured Laird Johnstone that Elsbeth was untouched, so he couldn't stride over to the man, wake him up, and tell him they were married.

He laid back down, sleep very far from him now. There was only one way to solve the dilemma.

He had to seduce Elsbeth.

He turned again, groaning as he rolled over a stone. 'Twould not be a problem if they weren't surrounded all day and night by her da, the man who thought she was his betrothed, and four of Duncan's men.

According to his calculations, they were going to pass either very close, or right through Grant land Freuchie Castle. All he had to do was find a reason he needed to stop at his keep on the way to Dornoch. If luck and his skills in bedsport were with him, he could bed the lass there, then announce to the laird that the deed was done, and they were married.

He slumped. What about Elsbeth? She was determined to return to Dornoch Castle. However, she'd been resolute to enter the convent also, but she wavered near the end, and he was sure he saw relief in her eyes when they found the convent had been shut down.

Another problem arose. He would be tricking her into marriage. He would get what he wanted, but at what cost? No cost if he told her he loved her. She was waiting for those words, which told him she must hold strong feelings for him.

He'd been holding himself back since he'd met the lass, terrified of ending up like his da if something happened to her if he'd succumbed to love. She could die in childbirth, could get thrown from her horse. Any number of things could take a life. Illness, a castle attack, a cut that didn't heal. He broke into a sweat and hopped up. 'Twas better to keep watch and let his men sleep since he wasn't going to get any with all this on his mind.

"Duncan?" Her soft voice rolled over him like honey as he made his way to where John kept watch.

He switched direction and headed to her tent, squatting before her. "Aye. Why are ye awake, lass?"

"I doona ken. I woke up a bit ago and canna seem to return to sleep. Why are ye up?"

"'Tis almost time for my watch."

She crawled from her tent, stood, and shifted her skirts. "Since everything is so quiet, can I sit with ye? mayhap we can even have a conversation without Mr. MacMillan barging in, reminding me I'm his betrothed."

"Which ye are no'."

"Nay. And I ne'er will be."

They wandered over to where John sat, and Duncan tapped him on the shoulder. "Off to bed with ye, lad. 'Tis my turn."

John nodded and left the two of them standing there. Duncan waved to the log that John just vacated and gave a deep bow. "Have a seat, my lady."

She curtsied. "Thank ye, my laird."

He sat alongside her and took her hand in his, rubbing the soft skin on her knuckles with his thumb. "Am I yer laird, Elsbeth? Am I anything of yers?"

14

Am I anything of yers?

Duncan's words played over in her mind as Elsbeth and the group of men departed the next morning and continued their journey to Dornoch. 'Twas a cool, damp day despite it being summer. A low mist lay on the ground, setting the scene for all the stories she'd heard as a bairn about fairies, kelpies, and brownies.

She shivered, remembering many nights when she'd been unable to fall asleep after hearing tales from clansfolk while sitting around the fireplace. She and Ainslee would huddle together in the bed, jumping at any unfamiliar sound.

No longer did she ride in the front of the group. Duncan and her da had claimed that spot with Mr. MacMillan continuously attempting to wiggle his way between them. John and Gregory rode alongside her and Kevin and Daniel in the rear.

"Are ye cold, lass? I saw ye shiver," John said.

"A bit, mayhap. 'Tis no' a pleasant day. I—" Her words

were cut off when she gripped Grisone's mane and clenched her knees as the horse stumbled, but she managed to keep her seat.

"Halt!" Gregory shouted. Duncan and Da turned, both of them riding back. "What's wrong, lass?" Da asked.

She was breathing heavily and was a tad shaken. "Grisone stumbled."

Duncan vaulted from his horse, then helped her down. Carefully approaching the skittish horse from the side, he smoothed his palm down the horse's nose and spoke to him in a gentle tone. Then he backed up and looked at the animal. "He is holding this front right leg up. He must have hurt himself when he stumbled."

"Ach. Does it look bad?"

"'Tis hard to say." He bent and ran his hand over the horse's leg, who pulled away when Duncan reached about three inches above his hoof. "'Tis no' broken, probably a pulled muscle."

He stood and placed his hands on his hips. "Ye won't be able to ride him."

"Lady Elsbeth can ride with me," Mr. MacMillan said as he joined them, his arrogant demeanor annoying her once again.

"Nay. She canna ride with ye all the way to Dornoch; 'twould kill yer horse," Duncan said and waved toward Grisone. "And this animal needs treatment. We canna expect him to walk all the way to the Sutherlands."

"She shouldna be going to Dornoch," Mr. MacMillan said. "She is my—"

"Stop!" Elsbeth shouted, her hand in the air. "I doona want to hear ye say that again." She moved over to where

Grisone stood and laid her head on the horse's face. "He is in pain."

"I have an idea," Duncan said. He looked at Elsbeth as if he expected her to begin shaking her head. "My castle is no more than a few miles to the west. We can get treatment for the horse there."

Elsbeth narrowed her eyes. If she wasn't the one riding the horse that stumbled, she would believe Duncan planned this to get her to his castle.

Before she even had time to think about what Duncan had said, Da squashed any objection she might have. "'Tis a fine idea, Laird. I, for one, am verra tired of traveling. I could use a soft bed and a hot meal. A cup or two of good Scottish whisky wouldna be refused either."

"I doona like this," Mr. MacMillan said. He pointed his finger at Elsbeth. "She planned this."

Elsbeth walked up to the man, her hands fisted at her sides. "Ye think I am such a poor rider that I would purposely harm my horse?"

Rather than answer, the man grumbled. "I doona trust him." He pointed to Duncan.

"Aye. And I doona trust ye, so I guess we have a mutual distrust." Duncan dismissed the man and returned his attention to Elsbeth. "Ye shall ride my horse, and I will walk Grisone the few miles."

It amused Elsbeth that with all the volunteering Mr. MacMillan had done, he didn't jump at the chance of walking the distance to Freuchie Castle.

Duncan helped her onto his horse, and they slowly made their way to Freuchie. He sent Kevin on ahead to advise the castle of their return and to notify the head stablemaster that they were bringing an injured horse.

Elsbeth had a strange feeling in her stomach when the castle came into view. When she'd left, she was certain she'd never see the place again and would spend the rest of her life in a convent.

The Lord works in strange ways, my lady.

Madeline, the healer at Freuchie, uttered those words when Elsbeth had told her of being taken from her group. Was the convent being closed and the horse being injured part of the Lord's plan?

Nonsense.

They crossed the drawbridge and rode through the outer gate. "Elsbeth, can ye find Bridget and make sure Kevin has told her we have guests? Darby, MacMillan, and yer da will need rooms."

"I doona need a room, lass. I'll be happy to sleep in the great hall near the fire. 'Tis more comfortable than I've been in years," old Darby said, looking around with appreciation, licking his lips.

"Aye." 'Twas such an eerie feeling to be back again. Since Kevin had been sent ahead, no one seemed surprised to see her. She wondered if the chatelaine had arranged for her to have the same bedchamber she'd had before.

As she made her way through the outer bailey to the inner bailey, Madeline shuffled toward her. She stopped and laced her fingers together and placed them at her waist. "I see ye have returned."

"Aye." There didn't seem to be much more to say.

The woman looked at her with a smirk that said she'd expected it. She patted her arm. "Ye will be happy here, lass. 'Tis yer home."

* * *

Duncan led Grisone to the stable where he met Graham, the stable master. "The horse stumbled. From what I could see, it was a small animal hole. I doona think it's more than a strained or pulled muscle, but he is limping."

Graham pulled on the brim of his cap. "I'll check him, my laird."

"Thank ye. And we have two other horses that will be added to the stable for a while."

"Aye, Kevin stopped by and told me. 'Tis Lady Elsbeth's da?"

Duncan nodded. "Be sure to take good care of the man's horse."

"Any particular reason why, my laird?" The man grinned in a way that both irritated and pleased him. "None that ye need to concern yerself with."

"What about the other one?"

He laughed. "I'd say ye can dump that one in the woods, but I want the mon who owns it out of here as soon as possible."

Duncan found Elsbeth standing in the inner bailey, staring up at the keep. He walked up to her and placed his hands on her shoulders. She turned slightly and looked at him as he wrapped his arms around her middle, resting his head on her shoulder. "I ne'er thought I would be back here." She chuckled. "I ne'er thought I would be here at all."

"Are ye certain ye want to return to Dornoch? Ye can stay here. Surely ye must be tried of traveling."

She nodded. "Aye, I am, but I have no place here."

Now was his opportunity. "Ye can have a place here. If ye marry me."

She turned in his arms, questioning him with her eyes.

"Unless things have changed since the last time ye asked me that question, the answer would be the same."

"Ye are still holding out for love? What about protection, bairns to love and raise, a comfortable life with someone who admires and respects ye?"

She sighed and offered him a soft smile. "We've been through this before. I've seen the glow on Ainslee's face. On Maura's face. If I canna have that, then I ken I will always feel cheated. I'd rather dedicate my life to helping others, even if I canna join a convent."

Frustrated, Duncan cupped her head in his hands. "Doesn't desire count? I'm sure the glow ye see on yer sisters faces comes from desire for their husbands."

She shrugged. "Mayhap that's part of it. But I also see the way their husbands look at them. Yes, I see desire, but I also see love. Either one of them would do anything for their wife."

He leaned back, his brows raised. "And ye think if I canna admit to love, I wouldna do anything for ye?"

Elsbeth closed her eyes and shook her head. "Ye doona understand."

His frustration was growing. He refused to be his da, so in love with his wife that he gave up on life when she died. He wouldna leave a bairn or two to fend for themselves because his wife was gone. Nay. He couldna do that.

'Twas time for a change of subject. "What do ye plan to do about MacMillan?"

'Twas Elsbeth's turn to look frustrated. She backed up, out of his arms. "I plan to do nothing about the mon. I've told him so many times I willna marry him, that my throat is sore. 'Tis up to my da to convince him that he is wasting his time."

"And ye are still determined to travel to Dornoch? To be where ye say it hurts to watch yer sister? Do ye think that's the best decision?"

Elsbeth hesitated for a moment, looking around the keep. When she turned to him, the tears in her eyes were obvious. "If ye will excuse me, Duncan, I feel fatigued. All of this is wearing on me. I think a short rest before supper will be best."

"Lady Elsbeth!" MacMillan strolled up to them, a scowl on his face. "I doona like ye spending time alone with Grant."

Instead of answering him, she growled and turned on her heel, stomping away. When MacMillan moved to follow her, Duncan grabbed the man's upper arm. "Doona even think about following her. If ye do, I will have to follow ye, and I can assure ye, 'twill no' be pleasant for ye."

MacMillan didn't move but shrugged Duncan's hand off his arm. "I doona ken what ye think ye will accomplish with this trip to yer castle. I'm allowing that Laird Johnstone has expressed a desire to rest from his travels and stay here for a bit, hoping to convince his daughter to forget this plan to travel to Dornoch." He poked himself in the chest with his thumb. "I intend to stay here until I wed the lass."

Duncan rocked back on his heels, studying the idiot. "Ye forget I am the laird. I willna allow ye to stay here more than a day or two, and that is merely to refresh yerself for the trip back to yer home. Lady Elsbeth has told ye she willna repeat her vows with ye. Ye are wasting yer time."

"I have a contract," MacMillan growled.

Duncan waved his hand. "Aye, but ye will ne'er have the lass, so I think ye ken what ye can do with yer contract."

Owen approached the two men. "Laird, there's a few things we need to talk about."

Duncan turned away from the annoying man. "Aye, Owen. Come to my solar." He looked at MacMillan. "I'm done here."

They were silent in their walk into the keep. Duncan would have enjoyed a cup of ale or Scottish whisky and a chance to forget everything in his life that brought nothing but annoyance.

He collapsed into his seat and rubbed his forehead. "That mon has gone from annoying to infuriating."

Owen took the chair in front of Duncan's desk. "It seems to me before I tell ye what went on in yer absence, ye need to explain why yer back here with the lass. I thought she was going to a convent?"

"Aye. That was the plan." Just thinking about the past few days raised his ire. "But when we arrived, the place had been closed down and the sisters sent to London to face some sort of charges. Charles is cracking down on convents all over Scotland, trying to prove to himself he's no longer Catholic."

"Can I assume that the lass is going to marry ye like everyone thinks she should?"

"Ach. 'Tis the problem. She is tired of everyone telling her what she should do. I've asked her more than once, but she has turned me down."

Owen's brows rose. "She thinks she can do better than Laird?"

"Nay. She wants love," he spit out. "Just the thing to tie a mon into knots and cause him to make foolish mistakes."

Owen studied him for a minute. "Like yer da," he said softly.

Duncan didn't answer him but stared out the window at the summer afternoon. The mist had cleared, and everything looked as it should. Except he was in knots.

"And who is that mon you were close to pummeling?"

"William MacMillan," Duncan growled. "He has some connection to the MacMillan laird. Lady Elsbeth's da signed a betrothal contract with the clan when he learned she planned to join a convent. He met us in Perth with MacMillan, claiming Lady Elsbeth had to honor it."

"And what did the lass say?"

Duncan grinned, thinking of all the times she'd told the man nay. "She told him nay in quite a few different ways and at different times." He slammed his hand on the desk. "But the arrogant mon willna listen."

"So where does that leave her?"

Duncan sighed. "'Tis her intention to return to Sutherland's clan where her sister is." He shook his head. "She's merely being stubborn."

Owen sat back, crossing his arms over his chest. "It sounds to me like ye are both being stubborn. I see the way she looks at ye and the way ye look at her. Ye might deny it, but I'm afraid to tell ye, Laird, that ye already love the lass."

Panic gripped him to hear the one thing he'd been afraid to even consider. Was he already in love with Elsbeth? Was he truly being stubborn?

"One interesting thing to note," Duncan said, "twice while we were traveling, someone referred to Lady Elsbeth as my wife. In neither case did we dispute it."

Owen slapped his hand on his thigh. "There ye have it, Laird! Ye are married."

Duncan held up his hand. "Nay. I have no' touched the

lass, so any marriage that resulted from our lack of denying it is no' legal."

"Ach, mon. Do I have to tell ye how to fix that problem? Bed the lass, announce yer marriage, and escort the obnoxious mon over the drawbridge."

There was that idea again. Duncan drummed his fingers on the old wooden desk and gave serious consideration to the plan.

* * *

"Elsbeth, may I speak with ye for a moment." Her da sat in the great hall, a cup of ale in front of him. He was surrounded by Darby and the four men who'd traveled with them. They all seemed quite friendly.

"Can it wait, Da? I'm feeling unwell." All she wanted to do was retire to her bedchamber and possibly never come out.

He waved his cup at her. "Ach, sure, sure, lass. We can talk later."

Darby thumped his cane on the floor. "Lass. Ye might want to seek out Madeline. She's a healer. A very nice woman. We had a conversation about my aches and pains." He grinned at her, and despite all that had gone on so far in the day, she had to smile back. The friendly little man was already fitting himself in. She had a feeling when the time came for them to leave and travel to Dornoch, Darby would stay here.

Mayhap ye should too.

She dismissed the thought as they were all so confused. She trudged up the stairs to the bedchamber she'd never thought to see again.

She took in her surroundings, realizing how much at home it seemed. It looked the same, smelled the same. Even more so than her bedchamber at Dornoch. She unbraided her plait and shook her hair out, rubbing her scalp. Reaching into the bag she'd traveled with, she retrieved her comb. She sat on the bed while she worked the comb through her hair.

What should she do with her life? She'd been in a turmoil of one sort or another since she'd left Dornoch.

A light tap on her door drew her attention from her thoughts. Hopefully, it wasn't Da. She really did not want to have a discussion with him now about Mr. MacMillan. She still hadn't had a moment alone with her da to learn why he made the contract. Her head started to hurt again as she crossed the room and opened the door.

"Duncan?" The man stood there, leaning against the doorjamb, his muscular arms crossed, looking like the devil himself had come to call. A teasing lock of hair fell over his forehead, his dark eyes eating her up. She took a deep breath as his handsome face did odd things to her insides.

"Aye. Can I come inside for a minute?"

'Twas a bit improper, but things had been improper for her for a while now. At least he was asking and not giving orders as he generally did. He looked so roguish, his full lips in a crooked half smile that made her toes curl. For some reason she felt danger—not the sort that would threaten her life, but the sort that would threaten her heart.

Before she could talk herself out of it, she stepped back and opened the door wider.

"Aye."

15

"Why are ye here?" she asked, backing up as he moved toward her.

Ignoring her question, Duncan reached out and gathered her loose hair in his fist, pulling it forward over her shoulder. "I love yer hair down." He lifted the locks and rubbed them against his cheek. "Ye smell like flowers."

She should ask him to leave. She should leave herself, run as far away from this man as she could.

Her lackwit feet remained planted firmly on the floor.

"Did ye want something?" She licked her suddenly dry lips.

"Oh, aye." His voice was barely above a whisper. "I want something. Something that only ye can give me."

She was starting to get very nervous. This was a different Duncan. Not the ordering her around, teasing and laughing with her Duncan. This as yet unkenned Duncan, merely touching her hair, raised so much heat, she felt the need to remove her clothes.

Indeed. Her clothes itched and scratched and felt binding, as if she'd suddenly gained body weight. Whatever was happening had to do with him. The way he touched her, the way he looked at her. How close he stood.

He moved even closer, cupping her face, rubbing his thumbs over her cheeks. "Yer skin is so smooth, so creamy. Ye are a beautiful woman, Elsbeth. I doona ken of anyone who compares to ye."

Trying to lighten the moment and gain some air since her lungs had seized, she said, "My sister. She looks just like me."

He smiled at her diversion. "Nay. I have ne'er seen Ainslee—isna that her name? But even if she looks exactly like ye, no one ever affected me the way ye do."

She shook her head, trying to make sense out of his words. "Duncan." She backed up so his hands dropped to his side. "What are ye about?" Was that her voice? She sounded as though a mouse had invaded her throat.

"I wanted to see ye, talk to ye." With each word, he moved closer until he was once again within a single breath. A breath she was having a hard time accessing. He reminded her of an animal on the prowl. Watching his prey, moving slowly, offering soothing words. She shivered, telling herself she should insist he leave.

He reached for her, slowly pulling her close, then wrapped his arms around her body, offering his warmth and strength. "'Tis time we decided what to do about us, sweeting."

She knew one day this would happen. There was simply too much of a draw between them. She'd felt it almost from the first time she'd been thrust in front of him on his horse after he'd dragged her from her tent.

It had only increased as she stayed in his keep, traveled

with him to Perth, and then back again. She was always aware of him when they were in the same room. She told herself it didn't matter, she would never marry someone who didn't love her.

Somehow, while she was muddling through her thoughts, he'd managed to loosen her bodice. Before she could protest, he bent his head slowly and covered her mouth with his. She inhaled sharply at the contact. Instead of pulling away, she leaned in farther, eagerly accepting his tongue as he swiped it over her lips.

His large hands took her head and held it gently as he ravished her mouth. He tasted of mint, ale, and Duncan. She gave a short moan as he pushed her dress off her shoulders. Then came her chemise that dropped, along with her bodice, to her waist.

Instead of feeling uncomfortable at being exposed before his burning gaze, the cool air was a comfort, a way to stop the heat building within her. She felt the need to push the dress and chemise to the floor so she could feel his hands on her naked skin everywhere.

He pulled back and whispered against her lips. "Ye have been driving me crazy for so long, *mo leannan*. 'Tis time I showed ye how much."

His lips moved from her mouth to her jaw, her collarbone, and then to her breasts, where he left soft kisses scattered over her sensitive skin. The man certainly knew what he was about.

Gently, he sucked on one breast, then ran his wicked tongue over the nipple. Her fingers threaded through his hair, the soft curls in contrast to the strong man.

She groaned and pushed herself closer to his mouth, inhaling deeply at the surprising jolt of pleasure that sucked all the air out of her body. His hand wandered to her other breast and teased the nipple, rubbing his thumb over it, which drove unfamiliar feelings right down to her core. "Ach, Duncan, what the devil are ye doing to me?"

He scooped her into his arms and looked down at her, the depth of something she was unfamiliar with in his eyes almost frightening. "Teaching ye about pleasure. Showing ye how good it will be between us." He carried her to the bed and gently laid her down. "I've wanted to be the mon to show this to ye since the moment we met."

He stared at her as he removed his leine and tossed it aside. He toed off his boots and stockings and slowly rested his body alongside hers.

Could one die of a pounding heart?

He gathered her into his arms. The roughness of the hair on his chest rubbing against her nipples brought another rush of warmth in the area between her legs.

"Ach, Elsbeth. Ye are so beautiful. So perfect." He stared at her. "I want to bring so much pleasure to ye that ye scream with yer release."

She had no idea of what he spoke, but she wanted to feel what she knew made her sister smile so much when she looked across the room at Haydon.

'Twas her turn.

She reached up and cupped his chin. "I dinna ken anything about this. My sister refused to share what I wanted to ken. Will ye show me what I should do to bring ye pleasure, also?"

The smile he gave her melted her bones and almost brought tears to her eyes. "Aye, *mo leannan,* we will pleasure each other." He bent to capture her lips again, driving every thought from her mind as another twinge of something exciting and thrilling raced through her body.

She wanted this. Ach, she needed this. And she knew it had to be from Duncan for it to matter. 'Twas time.

'Twas past time.

* * *

Duncan might have told himself he didn't come to Elsbeth's room for the sole purpose of seduction, but once she appeared at her door, with her hair cascading down her back, all his good intentions were lost. He'd wanted her almost the entire time he'd known her.

Her spit and fire, her softness, her caring, laughter, and willingness to help resulted in a woman who he would desire without her incredible features and form. Combined, he'd been lost.

His hand caressed her neck, collarbone, and settled on her plump breast. Her soft moan told him she enjoyed when he touched her there. Some women enjoyed it more than others. 'Twas what made joining with her so alluring. The discovery of all her sensitive parts. A journey he intended to fully enjoy.

His lips brushed her nipple, then he took her fully into his mouth. She arched her back, pulling his head closer. "Aye, Duncan, there feels verra good. Doona stop."

He chuckled. "I assure ye, lass, if I stop 'twill be for something even better."

"I like the sound of that," she said, her words coming out in soft gasps.

His mouth moved to her other breast, his teeth tugging lightly on her nipple.

"What are ye doing to me? I feel so strange."

Smiling against her warm, soft skin, he shifted over her and used his two hands to drag her dress and chemise over her hips, all the way to her ankles. She frantically kicked the garments off. "Ach, that feels better. I am so verra warm."

"Ah, lass. Just wait."

His gaze roamed from the top of her golden cinnamon hair spread over the pillow, all the way down her lush body. The nipples on her plump breasts that teased, begging for his mouth, the dip of her waist, followed by curved hips he intended to hold onto while driving himself into her moist channel. She was perfection. And all his.

Her moan was either from his words or because once he finished his slow perusal, he began to slowly kiss his way down her body, past her breasts to her soft belly, twirling his tongue in her navel. That made her giggle, a sound he'd never heard from a lass during lovemaking. It made him smile, too.

Elsbeth tossed her head. "I ne'er kenned something so simple could feel so good."

At last, his mouth met the soft, swollen lips at her center, surrounded by curly hair the color of a dazzling orange sunset.

She gripped his head, fisting her fingers in his hair. "Ach, Duncan. What are ye doing? I doona think ye are allowed to do that."

His smile turned to laughter. "*Mo leannan,* we can do anything we want to each other here in this bed as long as we both consent and it doona cause more pain than pleasure."

"Oh, my. Then if this is allowed, please doona stop."

More laughter. Elsbeth was just as fascinating stretched

out on a bed before him like a feast, as she was standing on her feet, eyes flashing, and giving him the rough side of her tongue. He'd never had so much joy with a lass as with Elsbeth.

His Elsbeth.

He kept his tongue busy as she moaned and tossed and turned, gripping his head, but not this time to drag him away, but to move him closer.

"Duncan. Something is happening but missing too." More gasps as she clenched her fingers tighter until he thought she would pull his hair out.

"I feel it coming on, but 'tis staying away." He hardly understood her garbled words as he felt her body tighten, and then she let out a keening sound and gripped his head with her thighs. He continued to lick and swirl his tongue until she finally collapsed and sank on the bed as if all her bones had melted.

He climbed up her satiated body and placed his lips on hers.

* * *

Elsbeth could hardly catch her breath, and then was immediately smothered by Duncan's lips. She could taste herself on his mouth and found it both interesting and exciting.

She tried to raise her arm to rest her hands on his shoulders, but her limbs were weak. She moved her head aside to get some air. "I canna even lift my hands," she said.

Duncan kissed her forehead. "Give yerself time to recover, sweeting."

After about a minute, her breathing returned to normal,

and she was able to run her finger down his face. "That was wonderful. No wonder my sister smiles so much."

Duncan laughed, but she hadn't attempted to make a joke. "I assume this is no' the end?"

"Nay, *mo leannan*. As soon as ye are feeling up to it, 'tis my turn."

She shifted and suddenly became aware of the part of his body she'd felt other times when he held her close but had never seen. Slowly, she moved her hand down between them and pressed her hand against his trews. "Shouldn't ye take these off?"

"Aye. 'Twas what I had in mind." He kissed her forehead again and hopped from the bed. She didn't think she could crawl from the bed, never mind hopping off. But mayhap once he had his release, he would feel just as lazy as she did.

Her eyes grew wide once his trews dropped to the floor. "Oh, my, Duncan. Do ye think this is going to work?"

He smiled and returned to the bed. "Aye, lass. 'Twill work. 'Tis been working since the beginning of time."

"With all the people around, I guess it has worked."

Duncan took her hand and brought it to his appendage.

"What do I call it?"

Another burst of laughter. "There are many words, but cock will work fine."

"Cock." She tried the word on her lips. "A strange word to be sure." She looked down at his cock standing proud and tall. "For a strange object."

"Enough talk." He shifted so he was partly covering her body, his elbows on either side of her shoulders. His long fingers played with her hair. "I dinna ken how much ye ken about all this, but ye may feel a bit of pain when I first enter ye. But 'twill ease soon."

She pushed the hair back from his forehead. "How do ye ken this? Have ye done this with other lasses when 'twas their first time?"

He shook his head. "Nay. An honorable mon doesn't take a woman's virtue without planning to make her his own."

He looked startled as if he'd said something he hadn't intended to say. The look was gone so quickly, she thought she might have imagined it. Then when he quickly moved his hips against her, all thoughts flew from her mind.

"Can I touch it?" She looked down between them. 'Twas a strange looking object. His cock. She had to get used to that word. As she stared at it, it moved, seeming to have a life of its own.

"Of course, sweeting. Ye can touch me anywhere ye want."

He grinned as she slowly moved her hand, then wrapped her fist around it. "'Tis soft and hard at the same time." She looked up at him. "Does it hurt when I squeeze it like this?"

His laugh was short and sounded almost painful. "Nay, lass it doesn't hurt, but ye touching me makes me lose a bit of control, which I will need to enter ye for the first time, or 'twill be o'er too soon."

"I like when ye kiss me, Duncan."

"My lady's command." Reclaiming her lips, he crushed her to him. She moved her chest back and forth, enjoying the feel of her nipples rubbing against the wiry hair that traveled down the center of his chest to where it grew thicker as it surrounded his cock.

"Spread yer legs for me, *mo leannan*. Wrap them around my waist."

She did as he asked, and he shifted between them, settling himself so his cock was against her center. Then she felt him begin to push inside her. At first, it felt strange, odd. Then as he continued it began to burn. "Stop. 'Tis painful."

He immediately stopped, but the sweat on his forehead and the groan that came from between clenched teeth made her wonder if it was painful for him, as well.

Before she could ask him, she felt the heady sensation of his lips against her neck. Then he shifted so he could reach between them. His clever fingers found that spot he'd played with before. She began to relax. He pushed in a bit farther.

She whimpered.

He stopped and ran his thumb in circles around her opening.

Then pushed in some more.

She let out a deep breath. "It doesn't feel so bad now, Duncan."

"Thank God." He kept edging in. "Tilt yer hips, *mo leannan*."

She did as he requested and found the part he was rubbing with his thumb was now close enough for him to press his cock against her. "Ach, that feels wonderful, Duncan."

He pushed in and stopped. With a quick plunge he shoved all the way in. She squeaked, her hands squeezing his shoulders. He held still, and she counted to ten and then gingerly moved. "'Tis all right now."

Smoothing her hair back from her damp forehead, he smiled at her. "Ye are even more beautiful here in my arms. 'Tis where I want ye to be always."

His movements began in such a way that she felt the rise of the wonderful sensations from before. She also found if she moved a certain way and pressed against him, her own pleasure increased. What had started out as easy, fluid motions, became more frantic. His thrusts were almost savage as he gripped her hips tightly. She'd never felt such a connection to another person in her whole life. Not e'en her sister.

She closed her eyes as she felt the rise of what she knew would bring her to where she felt she could once again fly. She matched his urgency with her own thrusts. She wanted to feel that again, trusted him to help her gain it.

Duncan wrapped his arms around her and pulled her closer. His panting and movements pushed her over the edge. She inhaled deeply and cried out. Within seconds he gave one final thrust and buried his head next to her shoulder.

Within seconds he must have realized he was crushing her because he rolled over and pulled her flush against him so her head rested on his shoulder.

As they attempted to catch their breath, she ran her finger in circles over his chest. Neither spoke as they lay there, just holding each other. Soon the sweat dried, and they were cold. Duncan leaned down and pulled the bedcovers up, settling them comfortably again.

Elsbeth turned her head and looked up, studying him. She explored his face, her eyes going from the sweat-dampened hair on his forehead, to his hazel eyes and the slight scar covered by a beard.

She reached up and cupped his jaw, running her thumb over his beautiful lips. Offering a soft smile, she whispered. "It seems, my laird, that our marriage is now official."

He shifted onto one elbow and stared at her, his jaw dropping. "What did ye say?"

16

Elsbeth scooted out from under Duncan and left the bed, dragging the bedcover with her. She picked up his trews and tossed them at him. Wrapping the blanket snugly around her, she walked to the chest in front of the window and sat. "I believe ye heard me correctly, my laird."

Duncan struggled into his trews and joined her on the chest. "Ye ken I heard ye. I guess what I mean is what did ye mean by that statement."

"I heard the references to 'wife' and 'husband' when we traveled back from Perth. I also ken that announcing ye are married or having someone else say it and not dispute it, allows for a marriage by Scottish law."

"Not completely, however," Duncan added.

"Aye. That is why I've been denying the desire between us. As long as we dinna consummate our irregular marriage, 'twas no' legal."

He picked up her hand and kissed her knuckles. "So why did ye no' stop me just now?"

Tugging her hand away, she stood, wanting to put some distance between them. The bedcovers dragged on the floor as she paced.

"Lass, why donna ye get dressed? If ye like, I can leave the room."

She allowed a soft smile to graze her lips. "Ye already saw everything I own." She walked back to the bed, picked up her chemise and dress and made quick work of putting them on.

Duncan walked up behind her and placed his hands on her shoulders. "What do we do now?"

She turned, tying the laces on her bodice. "Talk to my da. He can send Mr. MacMillan on his way."

"Is that the only reason ye allowed this?" Duncan said waving at the bed. "To get rid of the mon?"

Elsbeth rubbed her eyes and sighed. "One reason." She paused gathering her thoughts. "I've been doing a bit of thinking. If I return to Dornoch, I will have no place there." She looked into his eyes. "Which is why I left to join the convent. That hasna changed. I will return and find nothing there for me."

"Ach, lass, ye will always have a place here."

She tapped on his chest. "What about here?"

He placed his hand over hers. "I like ye. Verra much. I hold ye in high regard. I respect ye, enjoy yer company. I want ye to be the mother of my bairns." He kissed the back of her hand and stared into her eyes. "I promise I will be a good husband. I will ne'er disgrace ye by taking another woman to my bed. I will protect ye with my life. I will ne'er raise my hand to ye in anger." He sighed. "That's what I offer, Lady Elsbeth."

She tightened her lips and nodded once. "Aye." She

pulled her hand away and turned from him to walk to the window, tucking her arms around her middle. "What ye are offering me might no' be what I always dreamed of, but 'tis better than a lonely ill-fitting life at Dornoch."

What she dared not tell him was how she felt about him. That she was in love with him, and a life of one-sided love would be painful at times. But better than what she would have if she left.

He pulled on his leine, stockings and boots, then held his arm out. "Come, lass. We might as well speak with yer da."

She took his hand, ready to face her da and whatever came afterward. As long as they were together, she could deal with anything. If nothing else, Duncan was her strength.

* * *

HAND-IN-HAND THEY APPROACHED Elsbeth's da who sat at a table in the great hall, drinking ale and laughing and joking with Duncan's men. MacMillan scowled when he saw him and Elsbeth approach the laird.

"Laird, Elsbeth and I would like a word with ye," Duncan said.

The man turned, his brows rising when he saw them together. "Aye. I wanted to speak with my daughter anyway." He waved at the bench. "Have a seat."

"Nay da," Elsbeth said. "I want to speak with ye in Duncan's solar."

Something in their demeanors must have given rise to Laird Johnstone's suspicions. His lips tightened, and he stood. "Verra well."

MacMillan rose, smoothed his trews, and rested his hand on the sword at his waist.

"Ye are no' needed, Mr. MacMillan," Elsbeth said.

"I willna allow a conversation to go on among the three of ye without me there to protect my interests."

Johnstone sighed and pointed to the bench. "Sit down, mon. I can certainly speak with my daughter without ye hovering over us."

"Fine, then Grant stays here."

Elsbeth's da looked at Duncan with raised brows.

"Elsbeth and I both wish to speak with ye, Laird. Just ye." Duncan was growing weary with MacMillan and looked forward to when he could dump his arse outside the castle walls.

Johnstone gave a brief nod and looked over at MacMillan. "Stay here, mon."

Despite further protests, Duncan led the laird to his solar.

Once the three of them were settled into chairs, he cleared his throat. "Yer daughter and I are married."

Whatever he expected the laird to do didn't happen. The man didn't rave, didn't swing at him, didn't shake his daughter. He merely stared at the two of them. "When?"

Duncan explained about the trip back from Perth and how two different people referred to her as his wife, which he didn't dispute. Elsbeth then surprised him by adding that both the innkeeper and his wife referred to him as her husband which she didn't dispute.

"So according to Scottish law we're married."

Johnstone raised a hand and Duncan knew before he opened his mouth what he was about to say. "Ye told me the lass was untouched. According to Scottish law ye are not legally bound yet." His eyes narrowed. "Unless ye lied."

Duncan's temper flared at the suggestion that he would be dishonorable enough to take the lass and then deny it. He cleared his throat, but before he could open his mouth, Elsbeth raised her chin and looked pointedly at her da. "Aye. 'Twas true when Duncan told ye that. 'Tis no' true any longer."

The silence was overwhelming. Duncan waited for the challenge to a swordfight. He waited for the laird to throw the first punch. Whatever the man decided, he would not harm his wife's da in any way.

Then the laird slapped his thigh and burst out laughing. "Ye saved me a bushel full of trouble."

Duncan and Elsbeth looked at each other, surprise turning to smiles. "What do ye mean, Da?"

Johnstone walked up to Elsbeth, and she stood. He pulled her close in a hug. "Do ye really think I would have let that arrogant dolt marry ye? I had no idea how insufferable the mon is."

"Ach, Da," Elsbeth said and hugged him tight.

The laird walked up to Duncan and stuck out his hand. "'Tis a pleasure to call ye son-by-marriage, Laird." Then he ran his fingers through his hair. "'Twill no' go well when we tell MacMillan. Yer marriage contract held a lot of promises for him as well as his laird. Might as well deal with it now."

The three of them left the solar and found MacMillan leaning against the wall across from the room. He straightened and looked from one to the other. "I have a feeling ye are about to do something illegal."

"Come inside, MacMillan." Duncan waved the man in

and the three of them followed. None of them sat, and Duncan looked at Johnstone and nodded.

The laird studied the man's face. "'Tis sorry I am to tell ye the marriage between ye and my daughter will no' take place. I will send a missive to The MacMillan and advise him of the change in plans."

MacMillan's face turned red, and he fisted his hands at his side, leaning forward. "Nay! Ye canna break a legal contract."

Duncan moved to stand next to Johnstone. He leaned down toward Elsbeth and said, "I think it best if ye leave us now, lass."

She shook her head. "Nay. I willna be chased out. I am tired of being told what to do."

Blasted stubborn woman.

Johnstone held up his hands. "It canna be helped, MacMillan. While these two traveled they were referred to as husband and wife. Ye ken the law. They are married."

MacMillan replied, "Not unless he bedded her." He gestured with his thumb to Elsbeth.

No one said anything for almost a full minute. Then, MacMillan growled, "From what I'm seeing, 'tis a good thing then. I wouldna want a trollop for a wife."

The words were barely out of the man's mouth when Duncan's fist connected with his face. The man went down, but instead of continuing the fight, the coward rubbed his jaw and glared at Duncan, then turned his attention to Johnstone.

"Ye will be sorry about this, Johnstone." He rose to his feet. "Ye have crossed The MacMillan. There will be payment."

He turned to leave the room, and Duncan stepped in

front of him as he reached the door. "Ye will gather yer things and leave. Tonight. I will have ye escorted out of the castle and beyond Grant land. I will also see that the cook packs a meal for ye."

MacMillan shoved Duncan's shoulder and left the room. There didn't seem to be any reason to go after the man and continue the fight. He was just glad to be rid of him.

Johnstone rubbed his hand over his face. "I will be needing to return to Lochwood Tower, Elsbeth. I ken once MacMillan gives the news to his laird, there is a good chance they will attack."

"I will go with ye and bring my men."

The laird shook his head. "Nay, Duncan. Ye stay here and take care of my daughter. I would be grateful for some of yer warriors to accompany me back to Lochwood Tower. I have a strong force myself, but MacMillan's outnumber mine."

* * *

'Twas decided that her da would leave for Lochwood in the morning. Duncan had already notified half his men to be ready to travel with him.

They sat in comfortable chairs in front of the fireplace in the great hall. Supper was over, and they were alone in their corner, even though there were still clansfolk playing games and drinking.

"Do ye want a proper wedding, Elsbeth? We could have the priest marry us and then have a celebration. Ye do deserve it," Duncan said.

She'd thought about it after Mr. MacMillan had left with two warriors accompanying him to the end of Grant land.

'Twould be an easy way to announce their marriage. "I think having the priest come is a good idea, but we need to do it soon." She looked at him and laughed. "Unless ye wish to sleep apart."

Her husband's brows rose. "I will have him arrive tomorrow. I'll send one of my men to the Gordon Clan, right next to us. The priest serves this entire area but resides there."

"Aye. If he can come tomorrow, mayhap we can have the ceremony before Da leaves."

She was quite happy that the matter with Mr. MacMillan had ended and that her da wasn't upset with her.

Then why did she feel as though something was missing? As if there was an empty space inside her?

With having the formal ceremony and the celebration that followed, 'twas two days before her da left for Lochwood. Two days of, if not complete happiness, at least contentment and feeling that she belonged.

A FEW WEEKS PASSED, and true to his word, Duncan was the best of husbands. He made sure everyone in the keep knew she was the new lady of the manor. He had all her things moved into his bedchamber and kept her more than satisfied there when they retired.

They shared supper together on the dais, along with some of his men, going over their successes and failures of the day. Always he was solicitous and concerned about her welfare. He kissed her often and made love to her tirelessly, showing her new ways of enjoyment each time.

Most women would be thrilled at her life. Her husband

was wonderful to her, handsome, strong, and accommodating. Just about anything she wanted, he gave her.

Except one thing.

Once a week she made a trip into the village. Although there were plenty of servants to purchase what the keep needed, she liked to go and look at what was available. It gave her the opportunity to speak with the villagers, crofters, and farmers who as laird and lady she and Duncan were responsible for.

Women might have an issue with some things they would not care to discuss with the laird but taking the laird's lady into their confidence made it easier for them.

Duncan would accompany her, and they would stop at the village pub for some meat pasties and an ale. The clan loved seeing them together, and they caused a great deal of smiling and well-wishing as they strolled by.

"I'm sorry, *mo leannan*, but I cannot go with ye to the village today." Duncan joined her in the great hall as she prepared to leave. "There is a major problem on the southeast wall. I need to inspect it and have it fixed. I doona think The MacMillan will come here to retaliate over the broken contract, since I'm sure they're already giving yer da trouble. But I need to make sure the castle is strong, especially since I sent half of my men to Lochwood."

"Aye, I understand. 'Tis no' a problem. I will take Margaret and Bridget with me."

"I also want ye to take two of my men along."

"Do ye think there might be trouble?"

"I doona ken, but I'm no' taking a chance with ye." He cupped her chin and kissed her forehead. "Ye are my wife. I want to make sure ye are safe."

She sighed. Of course, she was happy with his concern.

"Thank ye, husband. I will be leaving in a few minutes if ye can have the men meet us at the drawbridge."

They all met as planned and mounted their horses. Duncan was there to help her onto her horse. The day was cool, with the slight wind forcing her to wrap her arisaidh closer to her body. 'Twould be autumn soon, and then winter, the darkest, coldest time of the year. But she enjoyed the comfort of hot stew, freshly baked bread, and desserts made from the fruit in the garden. She smiled at the thought of them sitting in front of the fireplace in their bedchamber together while she did her sewing. Or playing chess.

The four men she'd been familiar with from their travels had been part of the group dispatched with her da to Lochwood Tower. Although Oliver and Fraser, the men Duncan had sent with them, were certainly polite enough, she didn't have the sense of friendliness she'd felt with Kevin, Daniel, Gregory, and John as they made their way to the village.

They arrived at the village stable, and Oliver helped her down from Grisone, who had recovered from his injury. She was pleased to see Fraser helped both Bridget and Margaret down. They all walked to the center of the village square where the crofters and farmers were set up to sell their wares.

"My lady, I will see to visiting with the blacksmith to determine if he is finished with our looms," Bridget said.

Margaret added, "I'm off to the silversmith to see if there is anything new."

"Ach, Margaret. Doona ye think ye should wait to see if yer lad has bought ye anything?" Elsbeth smiled at the young maid who was seeing one of the lads who worked in the stables.

"That's exactly what I want to find out, my lady. I want to ken if he has bought something I should be aware of." She grinned as she ran off toward the silversmith's shop.

"I will be drifting from table to table in the crofters' area," Elsbeth said to the two men who had accompanied her. "Ye can go to the alehouse if ye wish."

"Nay, my lady. We are under strict instructions from our laird to no' leave yer side."

Oliver's words brought a warm feeling to Elsbeth's insides. 'Twas lovely to have a husband who cared so much for yer well-being.

She strolled to the various tables, chatting with the women and men who sold their wares. She picked up a small carved animal which almost brought tears to her eyes. Conall's wife, Maura, had been relieved when her da had moved into the keep where he could be cared for. He had crippled legs and spent his time carving little animals that sold at their village market.

She did miss her sister, but as things turned out, she would at least be able to see her. Life in a convent would have forbidden her any visitors. mayhap one day, she would be having a bairn of her own, and Ainslee might be able to travel and stay with her for a little while.

She complimented the man on his clever animals and moved to the next table. A wee lass broke away from her mam and headed toward the table with the carved animals.

"Lili, come back here, lass." A young woman turned from where she'd been examining cookery.

The wee lass stopped and looked back and forth between the very enticing animals and her mam. Someone screamed, and Elsbeth looked up to see a horse with no rider that seemed to be in distress racing down the path directly toward Lili.

Without a thought, Elsbeth and the lass's mam both raced for the child. Elsbeth scooped her up and shoved her into her mam's arms just as the horse ran into her, knocking her to the ground. An explosion in her head brought everything to a black halt.

17

Duncan sat with Owen in his solar as they discussed the problem with the wall. 'Twas not broken, but weakened, and they needed to get it fixed as soon as possible.

"Are ye concerned that The MacMillan will come after ye, then?" Owen asked.

Duncan leaned back in his chair and linked his fingers behind his head. "I doon ken. I'm no' familiar with the mon or his clan. There doesn't seem to be any reason for him to come after me, since 'twas Johnstone who made the contract with them. He canna send men here to take Elsbeth since our marriage has been blessed by the church, which I am sure Johnstone told The MacMillan as soon as he arrived home."

"I must say ye seem a happier mon since ye married yer lady." Owen studied him for a few moments. "Are ye finally willing to admit ye love the lass?"

"Nay!" He stood and walked to the window and looked

out at the men training in the lists. "I like her verra much, but I told ye before I willna offer love."

He was shocked to hear Owen burst into laughter. He turned to see the fool man was so overcome with hilarity, he was wiping his eyes.

Duncan glowered at him. "I doona see what is so funny."

"Christ's toes, mon. Ye've been besotted with the lass almost since the day ye dragged her here. Ye might tell yerself nay, but 'tis obvious to all who see ye with her that the answer is aye."

"Nay." Duncan took his seat again. "I canna love her. Ye kenned what it did to my da."

Owen frowned. "What does that mean? Yer da loved yer mam."

"Aye. And when she died, he was miserable. Took to drinking whisky day and night."

Owen pursed his lips in thought. "'Tis true," his second-in-command said, "but he got over it, and moved on."

"Pfft! Ye ken he dinna have it in him to continue living. He died on that battlefield because he dinna care if he lived or died."

Owen leaned forward and rested his elbows on his thighs. "Is that what ye believe, Laird?"

"I ken it to be true. He e'en set up an advisory group to help me should he die before I was old enough to continue on as laird."

Owen blew out a deep breath. "'Tis sorry I am that ye think so. I agree that yer da was verra upset when yer mam died. But he did come around, gave up the drinking, and took up his duties. In fact, to the point that when he left for that last battle, he'd been in negotiations with The Stewart to marry the mon's widowed sister."

Duncan just stared at Owen, all the blood leaving his face. His heart pounded, and he had to shake his head to clear it. This man was telling him what he'd believed for the last ten or more years was not true?

After a few minutes, when his heart finally calmed down, he said, "Then why did he arrange for a council to advise me?"

Owen shrugged. "Because yer da was a responsible mon. He kenned that there are no guarantees in life. He loved ye so much he dinna want to leave ye to handle all of this yerself." He waved his arm around. "Since ye were a mere seventeen years, he did the right thing."

Duncan slumped in his chair. His dad had loved. He'd loved his wife; he'd loved his son. He wasn't afraid of strong feelings. He didn't wish for death on that battlefield.

'Twas a relief because Duncan had been worn out trying to deny his feelings for Elsbeth. He had thought about not making love to her so often or moving her out of his bedchamber so he didn't have to watch her sleep. Anything to keep him from admitting, even to himself, that he loved her.

The entire idea seemed foolish now.

Suddenly, he felt as though a dark cloud he'd lived under for years had finally lifted. He grinned at Owen across the desk. "I love her."

Owen nodded. "Aye. The only one in the entire castle who dinna ken that was ye."

He felt the need to tell her right away. She'd gone to the village, so now that he and Owen had completed their business about the wall, he wanted to see her. Straightaway.

He jumped up from his chair. "I assume we're finished?"

The lackwit continued to grin at him. "Aye. We're finished, but I doona think ye are."

They both left the room and strode across the great hall. Just as Duncan reached for the handle, the door burst open, almost knocking him off his feet.

Oliver stood there, holding Elsbeth in his arms. Blood dripped down his sleeve, and he looked as though he was about to collapse. "My Laird, Lady Grant has had an accident."

His newly found heart dropped to his stomach. But years of training for the battlefield took over. Elsbeth would not die. He would not allow it. Turning to Margaret who had returned with them, he said, "Fetch Madeline. Quickly."

"Follow me up to our bedchamber." He turned and hurried through the great hall and up the stairs. He wanted to take Elsbeth from the man's arms and hold her close, giving her his strength, but not knowing what her injuries were and how they happened, he didn't want to pass her back and forth.

He whipped the bedcovers off, lest they get covered with blood. Then Elsbeth would chastise him. 'Twas amazing what thoughts go through a man's mind when fighting hysteria.

"What happened?" Duncan finally had the nerve to ask, wanting, and not wanting, to hear the tale.

"A horse went wild in the village square." He took deep breaths, trying to tell the story even though he was struggling. "The animal was racing directly at a wee lass. Lady Grant raced to the bairn, picked her up, and shoved her into her mam's arms. But then the horse was on her and knocked her to the ground."

Madeline came hurrying into the room, with Margaret

behind her, carrying the healer's basket of linens, ointments, and other items of her trade. "What happened to her ladyship?"

Once more Oliver repeated the story while Madeline looked over Elsbeth, gently touching her in various places. "Aye. What I need to do is remove the lass's clothes so I can see the damage."

Oliver backed up.

"Madeline, do ye need me?" Margaret asked.

"It depends, lass. Are ye gonna faint on me? If so, nay I doona need ye."

The lass swallowed a few times. "I doona think I will faint."

Madeline then glared at Duncan. "Are ye going to swoon on me, Laird? Or lose yer stomach?"

"Nay." He was busy studying his wife. She was pale, blood still dripping from the side of her head. There was a bruise on her cheek, and the sleeve of her dress was torn. He could see more blood there.

"Then the first thing we need to do is remove our lady's clothes."

Duncan began with her shoes and stockings, then Madeline cut the dress off her, leaving her in a thin chemise, which was a wonderful idea that Duncan never would have thought of doing.

Tears came to his eyes, and his stomach twisted when he saw her injuries. Besides the head and cheek injury, she had a bruise on her shoulder and arm. Madeline tossed Elsbeth's dress onto the floor and turned to Margaret. "Fetch hot water from the kitchen. Then go to my room and bring the basket of teas."

When Margaret stared at Elsbeth with her hand over her

mouth, Madeline shouted, "Now, lass. I need these things now."

"Aye." Margaret turned and fled the room.

Duncan couldna stop staring at his wife. He'd relaxed somewhat as he studied her chest moving up and down. "What do ye think, Madeline?"

"Ach, Laird. I haven't had time to examine her. She's alive, that's all I can tell ye now."

That hadn't helped. He wanted to hear she was fine, would recover in time. He ran his fingers through his hair and paced the room while Madeline went over Elsbeth's bruised body.

Margaret returned with the basket of teas. Madeline nodded at the lass to place it on the small table next to the bed.

"Laird, I need ye to find something to put on yer wife. 'Tis too chilly for her to remain in just this chemise. Her body has had a shock, and she needs to be kept warm. We canna wrestle her into a nightdress until I can determine what all her injuries are. We'll need some woolen blankets."

"Aye." Grateful to have something to do, he rummaged through Elsbeth's chest and retrieved two woolen blankets and a long loose garment he'd seen her put over her nightdress.

He laid the robe over her.

"Wrap the blanket around her feet. That will help to warm her until I'm finished."

Madeline examined each injury, then turned to him, "The horse's hoof hit her head, but because our heads are round, it only skimmed it. That's what caused the cut on the back of her head, and also why she remains unconscious."

"How serious is that?" He was almost afraid to ask.

Madeline shrugged. "'Tis hard to say. We willna ken until she wakes up. Then we can make sure all her senses are there."

He watched, helpless as Madeline sewed up the cut on her forehead and cleaned and bandaged her other bruises. Eventually, she looked up at him. "Yer lady is resting now."

"How long before she wakes up?"

As she packed her supplies, she looked up at Duncan with sympathy in her eyes. "I doona ken, Laird. That is up to the Lord. I suggest ye say some prayers."

He nodded. He barely heard Madeline and Margaret leave the room. He pulled up a chair and sat alongside the bed and merely stared at Elsbeth.

His wife.

His love.

Would he ever have the chance to tell her? To let her know that she had taken over his heart almost from the beginning? That he loved her so much it made his heart ache. Nay, the good Lord would not be unkind enough to not give him the chance to tell her what she meant to him.

The hours passed. Owen came to his bedchamber to tell him 'twas time to eat supper. He declined.

Shortly after, Margaret returned with a tray of thick soup, bread, and stewed apples in Scottish whisky. It still sat on the table as he continued to stare at Elsbeth.

He refused to let himself cry. If he did, it would mean he had given up. He would never give up. He stood and paced. He sat and stared at her.

"I doona ken if ye can hear me, wife. But I have come to my senses. I love ye. More than anything in the world. I need for ye to awaken so I can tell ye when I ken ye can hear me. I want to hold ye in my arms and ne'er let ye go. Then I will say it over and over." With a deep sigh, he stood again and paced again.

He wandered to the window. 'Twas a clear night, with the stars so very bright. Elsbeth would love them. He wished he could take her outside, all bundled up, and show her the stars and kiss her until her lips were sore.

Finally, his body took over, and completely exhausted, he climbed into the bed alongside his wife and held her hand. "Elsbeth, love, ye need to ken that I love ye, lass. So much that 'tis an ache in my heart. Ye are the best thing that has e'er happened to me. Please come back to me, *mo ghràdh*. My love. I should have said those words to you so verra long ago. But I was stubborn, stupid, a lackwit, and anything else I can think of."

He carefully placed his arm around her waist and fell into a deep slumber.

* * *

ELSBETH FELT herself float up from someplace peaceful and restful where she was happy and content. A place where she could see her mam, whom she hadn't set her eyes on for many, many years. But something pulled at her, making her feel as though she had to turn her back on mam and all the soothing warmth and comfort and shake it off and return. Where, she wasn't sure, but knew that someone was waiting for her. Someone she dearly loved.

A large, strong hand rested on her hand. 'Twas a familiar hand. Hard and comforting. She heard a voice that she recognized. Feeling happy again, she thought mayhap she could return to the comfortable place, even though Mam was no longer there.

But someone else was waiting. Someone who meant so very much to her. With a contented sigh, knowing she was safe, she slept.

A voice once again dragged her from the comfortable place. A familiar voice. She tried to fight it, wanted to return to safety. The voice wouldna let her return. It kept calling her, calling her his love. The voice was so very familiar, it made her want to leave the comfortable place to be with the man she loved.

Slowly, she opened her eyes. Duncan sat in a chair alongside their bed. Her first thought was the man looked terrible. Like he hadn't slept in days. Hadn't changed his clothes or bathed. His head hung down, and he mumbled something that sounded like prayers. "Duncan?"

His head moved up slowly. "Elsbeth?"

"Aye. I think so. Although I'm not verra sure since my head hurts like the devil. What happened?"

Duncan just stared at her, his mouth open. "Ye are awake."

"That appears to be so. Was I asleep? My head hurts something fierce."

He grabbed her hand and kissed it. "My love. Ye are awake."

"Aye, so ye've said. What's wrong with me?"

He used the back of her hand to wipe the tears that slid from his eyes. Why was her strong, warrior husband crying?

"Ach, my love. Ye have been unconscious for two days."

"Why? I doona ken. It hurts too much to think."

He took a deep breath. "Ye were run down by a horse in the village. Ye saved a wee lass from being trampled. Do ye remember now?"

She frowned. "Aye. She was a sweet little lass. She ran

from her mam, and then a horse came running toward her." She closed her eyes. "Ach. Remembering makes my head hurt."

"Donna think, my love. Just relax. Ye gave me quite a fright."

She tried to move and let out a cry. "My shoulder hurts too."

"Ye were hit by the horse on yer head, shoulder, and arm. Ye are quite bruised, actually."

"Can I have something to drink? I am verra parched."

Duncan stood and walked across the room. He picked up a cup from the top of the chest and brought it to her. "Here, my love. I'm going to try to lift yer head a bit so ye can drink."

Elsbeth took a few sips and moved her head aside. "I'm so sleepy."

Duncan stood and stripped off his clothes. She watched him, her eyes growing wide. "What are ye doing?"

"Donna fash yerself, love. I'm just going to sleep with ye."

She yawned and closed her eyes. "That sounds like a good idea, husband."

Duncan crawled in beside her, his warm naked body bringing her comfort. He didn't try to pull her close, which she felt bad about, but knowing how much she hurt in so many places, she was just happy to have him alongside her.

He linked his fingers with hers. "I love ye, Elsbeth."

"I ken," she said as she felt slumber calling to her. "I love ye too."

EPILOGUE

September 1659
Freuchie Castle

"Elsbeth, I doona like the idea of traveling that distance with two bairns. And now ye tell me we are looking at another wee one arriving in seven months."

Elsbeth finished dressing Noah, and then turned her attention to Harris who need help with his boots. "Please, Duncan. I haven't seen my sister in almost three years."

"Well, if ye and yer sister would quit having bairns so close together, we could have made the trip before now."

What he said was true. Ainslee was about to deliver her fourth wee one. Every time they planned to either visit Dornoch or have them visit Freuchie, one of them was with child and the husband felt it unsafe.

"I am well, husband. This time I doona even have the early morning sickness. In fact, since I was unwell with the other two, I'm sure this bairn will be a lass."

He said nothing for a few minutes. "Verra well. I ken ye

are missing yer sister, as I'm sure she misses ye. 'Twill be a long journey. The wee ones can't be expected to travel for many hours at a time."

"I ken. And we can stop at travel inns on the way there and back."

"My love, ye ken I will always do what ye want. Except when it's dangerous. We shall go to Dornoch providing we take a group of men with us."

Elsbeth picked up Noah and wrapped one arm around Duncan. "Thank ye, husband. 'Twill be fun."

Two weeks later

"Ach, I shall never make this trip again," Elsbeth said as she attempted to feed Noah and Harris with the wagon bouncing all over the road. "How much farther did ye say?" She reached over to remove a small rock—where the devil did he get that?—from Harris's mouth.

"Not long now, my dear. I'll send John ahead to prepare yer sister for our arrival. I'm thinking no more than one more hour."

"Praise the Lord!" Elsbeth hugged her two lads to her chest. Aside from being anxious to sit, eat, and sleep in something that wasn't moving, she was very anxious to see Ainslee.

When her sister was having her first bairn, Susana, Elsbeth was to be there to help with the chores involved in caring for a newborn. Because of weather, she didn't make it for the birth, which worried her sister.

Hopefully, they would make it in time for the new bairn to arrive.

Dornoch Castle was just as Elsbeth remembered it.

'Twas a little more than six years past that Elsbeth arrived with her sister for the wedding between Laird Haydon Sutherland and herself. The laird terrified her, and the sisters conspired to switch places at the wedding.

Things were a tad uncomfortable in the beginning, but eventually, it became apparent to everyone that Ainslee was a much better match for the laird.

The drawbridge was down, and they proceeded through the outer bailey and into the inner bailey. Having been forewarned of their arrival by John, Haydon stood on the steps of the keep. He held young Lady Grace in his arms while Owen and Finlay hung onto Ainslee's skirts as she stood next to her husband with a very swollen belly.

Her sister looked as though she would explode any day. Before the wagon had barely stopped, Elsbeth handed Noah to her husband and stepped from the wagon.

Ainslee attempted to hurry toward her, but Haydon stopped her with his hand on her arm. Elsbeth joined them on the steps. The sisters hugged, and both burst into tears.

Duncan walked up behind her, carrying Noah, with Harris holding onto his trews. "Laird." He stuck out his arm, and Haydon grasped it to the elbow, the usual greeting among the Highlanders. "Laird," Haydon repeated.

"What say ye we get all these crying women and bairns into the keep?" Haydon said.

"Tis a good idea."

Two weeping women, their arms wrapped around each other's shoulders, two lairds, and five bairns made their way inside.

They settled at a table in the great hall. One of the serving maids Elsbeth remembered from her time at the castle made her way over to them. "We have supper ready, my laird. Shall we bring it out?"

"Ach. I would like to refresh myself before we eat," Elsbeth said. "At least wash some of the road dust from me and the wee ones."

"Bessie, will ye please tell Cook that we will expect supper in about an hour?"

Bessie dipped. "Yes, my lady."

"Goodness, Bessie has grown since I was here last. She was about six and ten when I left."

"Aye. She's married with a wee one of her own. She wed Boyd McDowell. Do ye recall the mon? He delivers the peat to us and others."

"I do remember." She shook her head. "So many changes."

"I have something to share with ye, sister," Elsbeth said grasping Ainslee's hand. bairn grows within her body. Since I ne'er saw ye during yer other times, I kenned right away the difference in ye."

"Ye look as though the bairn is going to come bursting out any minute," Elsbeth said eyeing her sister's frame.

"Aye. I wish it would. I'm weary."

* * *

DUNCAN, Conall, Haydon, and his cousin, Malcolm, sat around a table in the great hall drinking ale and boasting of past victories.

"I guess The MacMillan ne'er came after ye for stealing his bride?" Haydon grinned the question to Duncan.

"Aye. Steal her we did. Only we thought we were taking

another lass. Lucky for me I made the mistake. I canna imagine being married to anyone else."

Conall and Haydon both raised their cups. "*Slàinte Mhath!*"

"Nay, in answer to yer question about coming after me," Duncan said. "A few months after The Johnstone left his daughter with me, we received a missive that he had worked out the matter with The MacMillan, so I assume there was no retribution on him either." He took a sip of ale. "Made Elsbeth happy, to be sure. She'd been fretting about it."

Conall looked over at Malcolm. "How are the negotiations going with you and The Ross's daughter?"

Malcolm gestured to Haydon with his cup. "Ask yer laird. I've been away for three days."

Haydon rested his forearms on the table. "We still have to work out more of the details, but we have come to an agreement."

Malcolm straightened. "And?"

"Ye will become Lady Maureen Ross's husband. She is the youngest of seven daughters."

Stunned silence followed.

"Aye. I think that is why the laird approached me about a match with one of my kin. He's managed to get all the others married off, and at this point, he just wants to see the last one settled."

Malcolm blew out a deep breath and sat back. "Is he not well, then?"

Haydon shrugged. "I doona ken. My thoughts are that he's looking out for the lass just in case. Life is dangerous ye ken, and his son who will be assuming the lairdship is trying to settle into marriage with his own wife."

Malcolm looked a tad apprehensive. "So 'tis done?"

"Aye. It is expected that the laird, his daughter, and the son and his wife will arrive in the early spring. Once they are here, we'll have the wedding. Part of our agreement was ye would gain some of the Sutherland land for yer own."

Malcolm straightened. "Truly?"

"Aye. I have the area marked off. We can look at it later. Ye'll want to build a house for yer bride too. I'll have the men help ye."

A scream rent the great hall, coming from the bedchamber floor.

Malcolm turned white as snow. "What was that?"

Bessie hurried down the stairs and flew out the door to where the healer, and her niece Helen, who was the clan midwife, lived in a small cottage in the bailey.

Haydon tapped his cup against Conall's and Duncan's. "'Tis the beginning of a long night."

Did you like this story? Please consider leaving a review on either Goodreads or the place where you bought it. Long or short, your review will help other readers discover new authors and make purchasing decisions!

I hope you had fun reading Elsbeth and Laird's love story. Want more Highlander romance? Look for the next book in the series, *To Vex to a Highlander*.

First impressions are not always real...

Malcolm Sutherland, cousin to Laird Haydon Sutherland has been offered the chance to marry the daughter of Laird Bryce

Ross. To entice The Ross into allowing his daughter to marry his cousin, Haydon has agreed to give Malcolm a piece of Sutherland land.

Lady Christine Ross is Laird Bryce Ross's youngest daughter and her da is anxious get her out of the castle. Especially since Christine's brother recently married and the two young lasses do not get along.

Looking forward to marriage and a new life, Christine is shocked to discover upon her arrival at Dornoch Castle that her betrothed is a man she met at the Highland Games the year before. She remembered him as judgmental, cold, and arrogant. Malcolm cannot believe his bride-to-be is the flighty, irresponsible lass from the Highland Games.

Is this a match made in heaven? Or in hell?

Click here for more information:
https://calliehutton.com/book/to-scorn-a-highlander/

* * *

You can find a list of all my books on my website:
http://calliehutton.com/books/

ABOUT THE AUTHOR

USA Today bestselling author, Callie Hutton, has penned more than 55 historical romance and cozy mystery books. She lives in Oklahoma with her very close and lively family, which includes her twin grandsons, affectionately known as "The Twinadoes."

Callie loves to hear from readers. Contact her directly at calliehutton11@gmail.com or find her online at www.calliehutton.com.

Connect with her on Facebook, Twitter, and Goodreads. Follow her on BookBub to receive notice of new releases, preorders, and special promotions.

Praise for books by Callie Hutton

A Study in Murder

"This book is a delight!...*A Study in Murder* has clear echoes of Jane Austen, Agatha Christie, and of course, Sherlock Holmes. You will love this book." —William Bernhardt, author of *The Last Chance Lawyer*

"A one-of-a-kind new series that's packed with surprises." —Mary Ellen Hughes, National bestselling author of *A Curio Killing.*

"[A] lively and entertaining mystery...I predict a long run for this smart series." —Victoria Abbott, award-winning author of The Book Collector Mysteries

"With a breezy style and alluring, low-keyed humor, Hutton crafts a charming mystery with a delightful, irrepressible sleuth." —Madeline Hunter, *New York Times* bestselling author of *Never Deny a Duke*

The Elusive Wife

"I loved this book and you will too. Jason is a hottie & Oliva is the kind of woman we'd all want as a friend. Read it!" — Cocktails and Books

"In my experience I've had a few hits but more misses with historical romance so I was really pleasantly surprised to be hooked from the start by obviously good writing." —Book Chick City

"The historic elements and sensory details of each scene

make the story come to life, and certainly helps immerse the reader in the world that Olivia and Jason share." —The Romance Reviews

"You will not want to miss *The Elusive Wife*." —My Book Addiction

"…it was a well written plot and the characters were likeable." —Night Owl Reviews

A Run for Love

"An exciting, heart-warming Western love story!" —*New York Times* bestselling author Georgina Gentry

"I loved this book!!! I read the BEST historical romance last night…It's called *A Run For Love*." —*New York Times* bestselling author Sharon Sala

"This is my first Callie Hutton story, but it certainly won't be my last." —The Romance Reviews

An Angel in the Mail

"…a warm fuzzy sensuous read. I didn't put it down until I was done." —Sizzling Hot Reviews

Visit www.calliehutton.com for more information.

Printed in Great Britain
by Amazon